PAST LIVES

T

wch

With best wishes

Richard
Preece

PAST LIVES

RICHARD PREECE

LUMINARE PRESS
WWW.LUMINAREPRESS.COM

Luminare Press
442 Charnelton St.
Eugene, OR 97401
www.luminarepress.com

LCCN: 2021904933
ISBN: 978-1-64388-603-9

*To Amber, My Inspiration, My Strength, My Partner,
My Muse, My Eternal Love.*

CONTENTS

Hypothesis

Each of us is composed of
our body and our spirit.

Our body is ephemeral and dies;
our spirit is eternal and lives forever.

Therefore, a single spirit could live
within multiple bodies over time.

Good and evil can therefore transcend
each lifetime.

Chapter One

To quote Charles Dickens, "It was the best of times, it was the worst of times" as I walked into the office of Gabriel Kardac on my birthday 1978.

It was a typically bleak and overcast November morning in Birmingham. The air saturated with carbon monoxide from the overcrowded motorways lacing through the city. Spaghetti Junction had only made the mayhem worse. I drove through the smog, contemplating my meeting with Dr. Kardac. I'd made my appointment a few weeks before when I'd reached my wall. I could no longer tolerate the chronic nightmares that plagued me, and having tried all kinds of medicines and remedies to no avail, I had researched hypnotists. Perhaps that could solve my affliction.

I had come across Kardac in the *Evening News* advertisement section, of all places.

Suffering from fears, phobias, or nightmares?
Gabriel Kardac can help!
Tel: 0121-232-9666

I hesitated on the doorstep and then stepped aside. Thoughts were flashing through my mind, casting doubts about what I was embarking on.

I decided on one quick smoke to settle my nerves.

As I pulled the pack from my coat pocket and lit my favorite Dunhill International cigarette, I looked back at my car, parked by itself on the deserted street. After nearly ten years, I still loved my Jaguar XK120; turning in my new Ford Capri in exchange for this sleek, sophisticated sports coupe had been one of my better decisions. Saturday morning: my favorite time of the week, cruising through the countryside with Robert Plant screaming through "Custard Pie" or the English Chamber Orchestra mesmerizing me with the intricate counterpoint of a Brandenburg Concerto. The hit of nicotine brought me back to why I was here…

Nearly fifteen years ago, I had been promoted to Professor of Urban Design at the University of Birmingham in Aston, largely in recognition of the praise I received for my design of the new Bull Ring Centre in central Birmingham. Major components of my design were incorporated into the final architecture, which was selected over well-renowned architects and urban development companies. The professional papers lauded my contribution to the design's "postmodern freshness, bringing a new look and feel to our depressed city center, and returning shops, pubs, restaurants to the heart of our beloved historic Birmingham." Little over the top, but high praise. Indeed, after it initially opened in 1964, it became the shining star of a revitalized Birmingham, but with the decline of the auto industry, increasing unemployment, and escalating football hooliganism, it was now more like the black hole of a depressed Birmingham. Over time, the posh shops and swanky restaurants had been replaced by discount shops, fast-food takeaway, and empty, soulless pubs. The middle-class shoppers and restaurant-goers had been overcome by the less desirable enemies of our society: tramps, vandals, and hooligans. Petty crime and random violence had become rife. On a Saturday afternoon, you were as likely to be confronted by mobs of football hooligans marauding the center on their way to and from local matches as to rub shoulders with cheery shoppers and chirpy children. During any evening, you took your safety into your hands, at the mercy of muggers and vagrants. The Bull Ring Centre was no more the shining star of Birmingham!

Recently, I had been honored with a fellowship in the Royal Institute of British Architects. This recognition was in no small part due to the influence and popularity of my series of published articles advocating the value of renovation and refurbishment of our grand old Victorian buildings over demolishing and replacing them with soulless concrete tower blocks.

During the 1960s, our cities had been devastated by a trend towards modernization, resulting in elegant old buildings being ripped down to make way for a concrete jungle. The Bull Ring Centre was a classic example, for which I now felt partly responsible. There were of course exceptions, where modern design resulted in dramatic and often aesthetic constructions. Coventry Cathedral was a great example. A city center almost completely destroyed courtesy of the Luftwaffe was now adorned with a jewel of modernism including the most gorgeous stained-glass windows. Though I could take no credit for that success!

So, from a career perspective, I was feeling like it was the best of times. I was also thrilled about my local football team, which had been close to my heart since I was a teenager. For those of you who are avid football fanatics, you will likely relate.

West Bromwich Albion, though not as well renowned as the Manchester Uniteds and Liverpools of the league, have always cherished a strong local support base of which I was, and still am, a member. "The Baggies" had been playing well this past year, with the incredible performance of "The Three Degrees": Cyrille Regis, Laurie Cunningham, and Brendan Batson. The moniker came from the R&B trio, due to the fact they were all Black and played like artists. In their first season, with Ron Atkinson as manager, they were closing in on the top of the First Division of the English Football League, bringing a thrill and a glow to my heart. However, the previous week I'd had a personal encounter with football hooliganism that brought it a little too close to home.

The WBA home game against Tottenham Hotspur was likely to be a hard battle on the pitch, but the battle commenced before the kick off, on the streets of West Bromwich. Spurs supporters had arrived early in the day and spent hours in the local pubs, only leaving at closing time (2:30 p.m. in those days) to run rampant and cause havoc on their way to The Hawthornes. The police were out in force with horses to quell the mayhem, which succeeded only until the fans were on the terraces. Just as the match was about to commence, a Spurs fan leapt over the fence onto the pitch and ran to the Baggies end, waving his Spurs scarf and taunting the home supporters. He was quickly escorted off by the local police, but the atmosphere was then like a powder keg ready to explode.

At halftime my friends and I were in the toilets below the stands, surrounded by Baggies fans; all good? Unfortunately, not! They took us for Spurs fans, as we had no scarves identifying us as local fans. Before we knew it, we were engulfed in a swarm of angry fans eager for revenge against their opponents. Fists were flying. One of my friends, John, ran and leapt over the turnstiles to escape the ground, while Simon and I were stuck in the middle of the searching mob.

Finally, and fortunately unscathed, we convinced them we were not Spurs fans but in fact Baggies fans. Subdued, one of the mob gave us each a Baggies scarf and told us to wear it for protection. My one and only encounter with hooligans was over, hopefully never to be repeated!

After the game, I had returned home to the beautiful house I had purchased in the wealthy neighborhood of Edgbaston thanks to a promotion and salary increase after being awarded my fellowship.

So, it would appear, that it truly was the best of times for me.

However, it was also the worst of times from two perspectives. Firstly, I was alone and felt an emptiness due to not being able to share my successes and my life with someone else. Secondly, the nightmares and sleepless nights were taking a toll on my health and happiness.

All of this had flashed through my mind as I realized I'd finished my second cigarette. Looking down, I took a quick glance at my Cartier watch and confirmed that I was still ten minutes early for my appointment, but as was my nature, I was compelled to be prompt when it came to time commitments.

I double-checked the office number—101—stepped through the doorway, and after closing the heavy door behind me, ascended the stairs slowly. I was on a dark staircase with old, peeling wallpaper either side. A dim light hung above the first-floor landing, providing little help in finding the steps before me. It was all a bit tawdry and not too encouraging; nevertheless, I was committed.

I turned on the landing and knocked three times on 101, with no reply. I tried the door, and it opened before me. This must be the waiting room? An old leather couch to the one side, a coffee table strewn with last year's magazines, a lamp-stand in the corner: these were the only furnishings. Anxiously,

I sat on the couch. I leaned forward in the hope of finding a magazine to bide my time. No such luck!

"You must be James?" I heard a voice ask.

The door across the room had opened without my noticing, and there, silhouetted, stood a short, rather rotund man with a monstrous comb-over, his pudgy face squeezed behind heavy black glasses.

"Yes, James Price. Dr. Kardac?"

"Alas, no, just plain old Mr. Kardac. But thank you for the compliment. Although in reality I have little time for doctors; from my experience most of them hide behind a title and have few original thoughts. But I digress. Please come in and make yourself comfortable; the armchair should suffice."

As I sat back in the leather armchair, he slid a small, round stool from his desk to my side. Removing his glasses, he looked at me quizzically, as though analyzing me.

"Have we started?" I inquired.

"We started the moment you stepped from your car. I was watching you from the window." He gestured to the bay window behind me.

"By appearances, I might conclude that you are a highly successful young man, Mr. Price. Wearing a finely tailored three-piece woolen suit and a very snazzy, stylish silken necktie. You arrived in an expensive sports car, smoke quality cigarettes, and wear a collectible wristwatch. You have about you the look of confidence that comes only from experience and success in life.

"However," he continued, "*appearances* are called such due to the fact that they are in the eye of the beholder and often reflect a different perception to the reality buried within. So, may I suggest that your outward success is not fully supported by an inner feeling of success. Am I correct in that assertion, Mr. Price?"

He had leaned forward, resting his elbows on his knees, his tweed vest slightly open with a gold watch chain dangling from his chest pocket.

"Yes, you are correct, Mr. Kardac. Although I have all of the external attributes of success in life, I still feel an emptiness inside. I long for a partner with whom I can share my life. Also, I am plagued by nightmares that leave me tired and listless. I sometimes wonder if the two could be related?"

"Indeed, they possibly, if not likely, are related. A troubled spirit manifests itself in a troubled life. Our spirit and our body are inextricably connected. The key is to unlock the cause of the spiritual discontent. The cause may be repressed subconsciously; it may be related to an event or events long past but never quite addressed. It is my job to find the key and unlock the door to your hidden angst. Once unlocked, it is almost impossible for it to remain an issue."

"So, where should we begin?"

"Tell me about yourself. Let's begin with your relationships; that is often a good place to start."

"Well, my relationships always seem to start off rosy and optimistic, then quickly slide into discord, repression, and misery. The last girlfriend I had felt like being in a song by Squeeze, 'Is That Love?':

> *Beat me up with your letters*
> *Your walk out notes*
> *Funny how you still find me*
> *Right here at home*
> *Legs up with a book and a drink*
> *Now is that love it's making me think?*

"So, I've pretty much given up on finding the right girl for me and resigned myself to living alone."

"I have often found that there is something in our past—a conflict, an event, or a painful experience that prevents us from enjoying healthy relationships. Perhaps that is the case with you? Hopefully I can help you uncover your past and enable you to open up.

"Let's do a little exercise. I would normally start with your life's major events or vivid memories that seem to stick in your mind and pop up occasionally. Whether they seem important or insignificant to you, they will help me focus in on what may be troubling you. The root cause of your nightmares may be deeply subconscious, and if so, you would likely be unaware of it. However, I'd first like to hear specifics about your recurring dreams. Close your eyes, take three deep breaths, then picture what is happening in your dreams and how you feel. Are you ready?"

"Yes. Three breaths. One, two, three."

"I'm perched on a pole of some kind high above the ground. The wind is blowing hard as I cling for my life to the pole. Then the pole sways, and I lose my grip and tumble towards the ground, awaking in a cold sweat.

"Now I'm in a cold, damp, and dark place, like a cave or a prison cell. The walls appear to close in on me as the confined space gets smaller and smaller until I cannot breathe. As the walls touch me, I feel the cold moisture and then awake with a scream.

"The worst, though, is the sword or large knife. I'm in some kind of a struggle with someone holding a long, sharp blade as they lunge towards me. I try to evade the blade, but eventually it slowly pierces my chest, and I feel it sliding into me. There is no pain, only a grim feeling of hopelessness. Then, as with the others, I awake with a terrified yell."

"How frequently do these dreadful dreams torment you?"

"Almost every night now. Rarely will I sleep through the night without at least one of the nightmares."

"Now then, let me hear about your memories. Please don't analyze or process your thoughts, but simply share whatever comes into your mind. Let's start with your childhood; what events come to mind? Let's begin.

"Close your eyes and relax. Take a slow, deep breath in through your nose; hold it as I count to three. One, two, three. Now, let it out slowly through your mouth. Good. Now I want you to repeat that as I count down from ten. As you breathe, focus on your breath and clear your mind."

As he counted down, at first my mind was racing with thoughts popping in and out—mundane things like my grocery list, my lecture on the following Monday, my neighbor's cat—then the thoughts slowed, and as he reached "three," I was shifting into the past.

"Imagine you are there in the past, and describe what you see and feel."

"It's dark and drizzly as I am walking down Friar Street in Worcester with my brother. We're both wrapped up warm in our duffle coats, long wool school scarves wrapped around our necks. My nose is running as the cold wind blows in my face.

"'Let's try here.' My brother grabs my arm and pulls me towards the front door of the Cardinal's Hat pub. 'Your turn.'"

"Just inside the front door, I'm knocking on the opaque glass of the off sales window with my chin barely above the counter.

"As it slides open, I'm confronted by a rather large lady.

"'What d'you want, love?' she asks, laughing. 'Bit young for a beer, I should say!'

"'Do you have any beer mats you could spare, please? We collect them.' This was my usual line.

"'Of course, my little love, let me 'ave a looksie.' She turns towards the bar behind her and reaches down.

"'How's about these?' she asks as she reaches out and puts a handful of beer mats in my hand.

"'Thank you very much. These are lovely!' I smile and show them to my brother.

"We both take a look through them, sniffing the used ones, soaking up the smell of beer.

"'Well done, titch. Let's go and get some batter scraps at the chippie and head home; it's getting late.'

"I'm smiling broadly as I push the trophies into my coat pockets.

"It's fading away now."

"Interesting. Take another three deep breaths, and let's see what comes up next."

"Now I'm walking through the cathedral. It's quite dark, and I guess it must be after choir practice. It feels pretty spooky. I pick up my pace to get to the main door and outside. I stop and look at one of the tombs; it's massive. An angel holding a spear looks down at me. The inscription reads, 'Orlando Pryce, Rest in Peace. Cathedral Organist and Master of the Choir. Died nearby 1666. May God save his soul.'

"A shiver runs down my spine and my hair tingles as I nearly run to the door and bolt out into the courtyard to the safety of people, cars, and buses."

"Okay. That's good. Now one more time before we move on, please. Deep breaths."

"Now I'm running through an orchard. Looks like apple trees. Ahead of me looks like a hopyard. The grass is long, and as I run, I watch out to avoid the apples on the ground. It must be autumn. I head down an archway of hops. I can smell the pungent fragrance. I'm happy and feel at home somehow. It's a strange feeling, like I've been here many times before. That's it. It's gone now."

I opened my eyes and blinked a few times as the bright sunlight from the window blinded me.

"What does that all mean? I haven't thought about those things for years!"

"Well, it's quite natural. When you reach a deep state of relaxation, long forgotten experiences often come forth. Do you recall those events now?"

"Yes, very clearly. Each of them happened when I was quite young. I was in the Cathedral Voluntary Choir with my brother, and we would often stop at pubs on our way home after practice to add to our collection of beer mats. It was the best of times. A few years later, I got into the actual Cathedral Choir; the Voluntary Choir was pretty good, but basically local kids, whereas the Cathedral Choir was very serious. One of the best in the country. I had to take tests to get in. But anyway, it was a hard life with practices every morning and evening and services every night. After the evening service, I had to walk through the cathedral by myself, and I can tell you it was quite scary! I hadn't thought about that tomb before though; that's odd.

"As for the last one, I used to love exploring local orchards, looking for apples and playing games in the hopyards. I can still smell the hops like it was yesterday."

"But you also said it felt like you'd been there many times before; did that mean anything to you?"

"Well I did go there a lot, but the feeling was different, almost like I'd been there in a distant past. Which doesn't make any sense to me."

"Tell me more about the first story. The pub, the Cardinal's Hat, does that have any significance to you?"

"Well, it was the closest pub to the cathedral, so we'd often stop there first. Quite a few of the men from the choir would go there after practice, and I think the organist would often be there too. Not sure that means anything, but I did love that pub; it was always warm and welcoming, somehow. Like I felt at home there? Odd. It's still there. It was renamed to the Coventry Arms for a long while, but now it is back to being The Cardinal's Hat. It's the oldest pub in Worcester."

"It's not odd, really. It was a fond memory for you and at a time when you felt safe. Now, tell me more about the tomb."

"Well, that certainly wasn't a time when I felt safe! I used to dread having to walk through the cathedral after dark. But I have no clue where the memory of the tomb came from. I don't even remember the name—who was it?"

"Orlando Pryce. I wrote it down. Means nothing to you at all?"

"No. I've never heard of him."

"Hmm. Very interesting. I think we may want to dig a little deeper, if you are up for it?"

"Like how, do you mean?"

"Hypnosis. Let's dig deeper into your subconscious and see what comes up. Past events play a significant part in your current emotional state. Often, we are unaware of them, but they continue to influence us. Our conscious memories we can analyze and explain, but our unconscious memories need to be uncovered in order to analyze and explain them. Let's try hypnosis.

Richard Preece

"I will ask you to relax completely and then calm your mind, letting go of your current thoughts and allowing your mind to drift back to wherever it wants to take you. Your mind wants you to be happy and healthy, but at times it needs help to uncover and release repressed feelings. This we can accomplish during a hypnotic state.

"Are you ready? There is nothing to fear. Just relax and allow me to lead you.

"Let us begin…

Kardac continued. "During our hectic modern lives, we enjoy very cerebral pursuits…it's all too common for us to get 'up in our heads.' Swirling thoughts, anxiety, and stress. These can be controlled and soothed by reconnecting with our bodies. Direct your awareness to your body, part by part.

"Start with your neck and shoulders. How do they feel? Sense the tension in your muscles, and allow it to dissipate. You may be surprised at how much tension you are holding without being aware!

"Now move to your back and do the same thing. Next your face, your arms, and your legs.

"When you have finished scanning your body and are fully aware of it, it's time to shine the light of your awareness inward—to your emotions and thoughts. Allow yourself to recognize any major emotional or life events that are occurring at the moment. There's bound to be something, right…even if it's just feeling wound up at your boss after a long day at work.

"We're often taught that meditation is about 'emptying your mind.' Not so. Don't feel guilty for having thoughts!

"Mindfulness is more about how you respond to your thoughts. We are not trying to drain our thoughts away, like water out of a bathtub. We are merely allowing ourselves to recognize our thoughts and emotions without becoming attached to them. We are accepting them, casually observing them—and allowing them to pass, without focusing on them.

"Breathe naturally. Calmly. Allow each breath to slowly take its course. Focus your awareness on these breaths, feel every detail of them. One by one. Where is the breath in your body? How does it feel? Is it a long breath or a short breath? You may never have considered any of these questions before. But every single breath is as intricately and subtly different as the grains of sand on a beach.

"Each grain of sand comes from a different rock or perhaps a shell that was once a living creature swimming in the ocean. These details are often overlooked. Just as every breath is different.

"Our breath changes according to our emotional state, heart rate, excitement, and stress level. Feel it flowing over every single millimeter of your windpipe. Truly appreciate each breath.

"Count the breaths. From one to ten. Focus only on the breath. Allow any thoughts that intrude to flow away like water in the flowing stream. You may be surprised by how hard it is to simply count from one to ten without an external thought intruding! Do not feel bad, this is quite normal.

"Do this three times, for a total of thirty breaths.

"You are now in a calm, relaxed, and 'half-asleep' state. Your mind is alert, but your body is deeply relaxed and preparing for sleep.

"You are now ready to commence your visualizations. Let your mind go where it desires, and as it does so, describe to me what you see and what you feel…"

Chapter Two

OWEN REES

(1356–1416)

As my eyes open, I am walking along a dry dirt path-way with tufts of grass growing on either side blending into wild hedgerows. I hear a clinking sound and look towards it as my focus clears. There walking a few paces ahead of me is a short, squat man wearing a heavy brown wool robe with two tin mugs hanging from his rope belt. His bald head gives it away; he must be a monk. Humming to himself, he paces forward with a jaunty gait.

He turns his head, smiles, and calls back to me.

"Cum on, Owen, get a move on, else we'll never make it to the pub! My throat is verily drier than a nun's tit and my cheeks caked with Kentish crap. I'm a man urgently in need of an ale…or six! Hah!"

"Lord bless you, Friar Thomas. You've the tongue of the devil, but a true heart of gold. You'll get your ale soon enough, I'll wager. Look, there's the Cross Keys ahead, no more than a stone's throw. A sumptuous supper, a buxom barmaid, and a cozy cot await us."

"My you've a way with words. Me thinks we lost a poet when you took up your calling as a pardoner. Though more money in it, in truth. Your fine threads would be rags and your belly empty; speak not of the women you lay. You'd hardly get a hag! 'Tis a pardoner you are, through and through."

"Can't argue with that, Friar Thomas. Selling bones and scraps of fabric for pardons is a fine business to be sure. No shortage of scraps to sell, and no shortage of fools to buy 'em!"

Looking down, I am wearing soft leather boots and light grey tights under a long royal blue silk robe embroidered with gold twine. As I reach to my shoulder to adjust a large leather bag hanging on my back, I notice my hands are encased in smooth suede gloves. Swinging the bag from my shoulder, I take a peek inside to see all kinds of broken bones and scraps of fabric jumbled up together. There's a black leather pouch. As I shake it, I recognize the jangle of coins; lots of coins!

The Cross Keys is crowded. Our group of pilgrims happily quenches our thirsts after the long day's walk from Rochester. There's the knight always wearing his Red Cross despite the fact he hasn't seen combat in many a year! The Nun's Priest is deep in conversation with his friend the summoner , while the miller, short and squat with that enormous wart on his nose, leans over the table towards the prioress looking as innocent as ever as she sips her cup of water. The merchant, shipman, and cook are at the bar deep in conversation about business ventures, I'll warrant. The group looks well at home in the warmth of the pub.

There are no seats left in the pub, except at the knight's table, but neither of us are in the mood for his pontification and endless tales of his crusading exploits. So, tankards brimming over with ale in hand, we head back outside to the bench by the front door. Settling down in the early evening sun, we swig our ale and both sigh.

"'Twas a long day today, was it not, my friend?"

"Aye! But all the better for a beer!"

"I'll drink to that forsooth."

"So, tell me about yourself, young Pardoner, where is home for you, my friend? I'm eager for a little storytelling."

"Well, can't say as I have a home now, verily 'tis where I lay my hat. But I am still a Worcester lad at heart. Growing up under the bells of the Holy Cathedral of Saints Wulfstan and Oswald was a wonderful thing. Poor we were, though my pa was a wool merchant by trade; times was harsh and even worse when our glorious King Richard's advisers inflicted the poll tax on us in 1377. A whole shilling for every man, for heaven's sake. 'Twas daylight robbery, it was. But I got a bit of work on the tower for nearly a year. Hard labor mind you, hauling huge blocks of stone up them ladders day in, day out. My hands was like leather, as rough as all get-out. Used to end the day with a lovely pint of ale at the Cardinal's though; that was magic! That was where I met Hal."

"Who was Hal?"

"Oh, we was both poets, or so we thought, and used to play games making rhymes about the locals in the pub. Good times, they was. Hal had been in the rebellion in Essex and marched on London with a gang of ruffians. Burned down old John of Gaunt's palace, they did. He was right there in the thick of it. Then old John fled with his tail between his legs off to Scotland, I believe. Hal said he even met the king at Mile End, but he was one for tales, so I took that one with a shovel of salt! But it all fell apart when Wat Tyler was murdered in cold blood by that bastard mayor of London. Then the king lavished on his favorites, Michael de la Pole and Robert de Vere. Hal said that was enough and headed off to Worcester to start a new life and work on the tower. That's how we met. Nice lad."

"Sounds like a character indeed!"

"Aye, he was. He was the one got me into pardoning. 'You're a master at tales,' he says. 'Why not grab a few bits of stone from the mason's yard and sell 'em off as blessed relics from Oswald's tomb?' Got me thinking, it did! And right as rain, I was making myself a nice living on selling anything I could lay me 'ands on. Pigs bones was saint's bones, bits of rags was sacred garments. Easy living."

"But why do they buy them?"

"Ah! That's the trick. They call me the Pardoner for good reason. I tell them that if they purchase a sacred relic, their sins will be pardoned. Can't go wrong! Fools will believe what they want to believe."

"You're as slippery as a snake, young Pardoner. I'll warrant you're closer to the devil than you might wish. But enough serious talk. Let's get another ale afore it's time for supper."

So off we go back to the bar to replenish our tankards and go our separate ways: the Monk to chat up the Nun's Priest and myself towards the fireplace, for though it is late summer, my bones feel chilled.

As I sit staring into the glowing embers, I feel a shiver run down my spine. I look up to see a gentleman standing just across from me by the fireplace. Anachronistic in our close group of pilgrims, looking out of place in his finery. Who is this?

Dressed in cloth the like of which I've not encountered and with a confident swagger, he gestures to me as he walks across the bar.

"Hail, Mr. Pardoner! Prithee let me join you in your solace."

"Who art thou that knows me without knowing me?"

"I am thy benefactor."

"Benefactor? I know not thou!"

"Not as yet, perchance, but surely, thou shalt given time and good fortune."

"Good fortune for whom, I say!"

"For thou, in truth. If thoull'st give me thy time."

"My time is my own, though an ale would surely come natural. What say you?"

"Cheap thou art, Pardoner. Why not a mead for my tale?"

"Thy tail be between thy legs, forsooth!"

"'Tis more true than thou knowest."

"A mead it is."

As he sits beside me on the wooden stool, I look at him in all his glory. Fine clothes. And a manner I've not seen. A foreigner for sure.

"Who art thou, fine fellow?"

"They call me Bernael. My full name being quite a mouthful: Bernael Constantine Le Ciffre."

"Not from these parts, I'd wager?"

"Indeed, I have traveled far and wide. Though I've found that nothing really changes. Men are men wherever they're from."

"I'll drink to that! A man's a man for all that. And verily a woman is the same."

"How is the pardoning business?"

"And how do you know such things? Am I a pardoner or a friar?"

"I know you well, Owen Rees. You make petty pardons for paltry change when you could be living a life of luxury. What is it you most desire?"

"Wine, women, and song! What else is there?"

"Much more, my friend, much more."

"So say you!"

"In truth, I'd wager your wine is watered and your women cheap."

"So, what of it?"

"You could do better. I can offer you the most delicious wines and the most sumptuous women of your imagination. More than you could dream."

"Who are you that you can offer that to me?"

"That is for me to know. Mark my words, Owen. I have power beyond your imagination. Doubt me not."

"So, what's in it for you? In my trade I'm well experienced with selling falsehoods."

"Simply put, Mr. Pardoner, your soul. Which I venture you may have already sold?"

"Not I. My soul, for what it is worth, is mine and mine only."

"Do you value it so?"

"Value it? Not I! I am for this life alone. I may sell the hope of redemption with fake bones and rags, but I believe in it not. My only belief be in such that I can touch, taste, and see. Nothing more."

"Then you may consider my proposition."

"Proposition? I'm all ears for propositions. Now you're talking my terms."

"Hear ye then. I will guarantee you a life of everything you desire: wine, women, wonderment, all that you could possibly desire. In exchange for one small thing."

"What be that then? What do I possess that could be of interest to you?"

"Your soul."

"Hah! My soul? That be worthless. Take it. It's yours."

"Heed my words afore ye make jest. Casting your soul aside is eternal. This life's pleasures are little in comparison."

"This life is all there is. Short and shitty! All there is."

"So be it then. It seemeth to me we have a deal, Mr. Pardoner."

"Forsooth, a better deal I never made!"

He reaches into his side pocket and pulls out a scroll wrapped in black ribbon. Untying the bow, he unrolls it before me. To all intents, it appears alike my contracts of verification for my religious artifacts. Nothing I've not signed a thousand times.

The last sentence being the only difference:

"On thy sixtieth birthday thou shalt meet me at the Tabard Inn, Southwark, at such place concluding our arrangement to this end."

He passes me a quill and an ink well in shiny silver.

"So be it then." I sign my full name: Owen James Rees.

"See you at the Tabard then!"

"Then the deed is done! May I offer you a drink in celebration of our contract?"

"Aye! Another mead would suffice."

As I slurp down my mead and wipe my lips, I look up and he's gone.

The bar fades and then just like watching a movie or a dream, I see a series of flashes: scenes of debauchery, women of all shapes and sizes (mostly as nature made them), casks of ale and flagons of wine, cloth bags of jingling coins dropped on tables, and a casket filled to the brim with supposed relics.

Then the scenes slow down and I'm seated again. This time in a different pub. Definitely a pub, though unfamiliar. I'm sitting next to a crusty looking young man dressed in a leather waistcoat and sipping his ale.

"So, it were unimaginable. Hordes of them there froggy knights fully clad in shining armor hurtling towards us. Lances tilted and at full charge. Shitting my pants I were, boyo. I 'ad me longbow now at full stretch ready to let loose. 'Hold, hold, hold,' I hears. For Jesus' sake I's thinking; we'm dun for. 'Loose.' Finally, all of us archers let loose as one. Time stopped, and all I heard were the whistle of arrows and feathers and the thunder of hooves. I looks up and there's like a cloud suspended in the sky, a cloud of arrows. When that torrent hit, it's like time started again. Them knights dropped like flies they did, so help me god!

"'Loose.' Another round. And another. Then all goes quiet, but for horses whining and men groaning. 'At 'em, lads. Finish 'em off.'

"Pulling our knives out, we charged into the mayhem. Knights was crushed under their mounts, some drowning in the mud, others struggling to stand up in amazement. We was in amongst 'em like flies, jabbing and thrusting. It's a gruesome thing, searching for that open spot betwixt helmet and breastplate and pushing yer knife in hard, feeling gristle and the blood spurting. 'Twas all over in a thrice. The whole lot of 'em, the flower of France, dead or dying.

"That was Agincourt. Bloody and nasty. But by god it were glorious!"

"You was there?"

"Aye, along of many of me mates from the valleys. Welshmen won it! I even got a glimpse of King Hal; lovely lad he were. One of us."

"So, what you be doin' 'ere this night? Ain't made your acquaintance afore."

"Verily, I say I'm a celebrating."

"What, may I ask?"

"Ah! 'Tis my birthday, and I thought I'd venture to new waters."

"Won't find no new waters 'ere; same old piss they pass off as ale! Hah. But I've a'been coming to the Green Man a'since I was a youngster, and it's my local and that's that. But I'm forgetting myself; let me buy you a birthday beer. How young is you by the way?"

"Sixty years young and not a day less!"

"Well my! I'd taken you for a youngster. Must be the clean living! Hah! I'll drink to that, my young archer."

As he stands up and turns towards the bar, I catch a glimpse of a familiar figure, and my heart turns to stone. It's him: Bernael Le Ciffre! Staring across at me with a perplexed look on his face. He lifts his hand in recognition and walks towards me.

"Now I'll be damned! Well actually I already am…many times over." He laughs. "I was thinking you and I had an appointment at the Tabard tonight, but here you are. Fortuitous. Saves me an arduous coach trip."

"Well…well that must have slipped my mind." I was quaking to the knees.

"Never mind. I was here on other business, which has now been adequately addressed, and so I am all yours. Or should I say you're all mine! Forgive the quip, but I cannot help myself. 'Tis time. Come with me."

I feel myself lifted from my seat and drawn towards him as he beckons. The faces fade and the room dims as I drift.

"Our agreement is settled in full."

Those are the last words I hear as the bar transforms to a sea of wretched faces and writhing bodies, clawing and grabbing at me, dragging me into darkness.

Chapter Three

⸻✕⸻

"As the vision starts to fade, begin to let go and return your focus to your breathing. Deeply breathe in through your nose, hold for a count to ten, and now breathe out through your mouth. Let's repeat that two more times…"

As I breathed in and out, the scene faded and I returned: first feeling the chair with my hands, then noticing my feet on the floor, then slowly opening my eyes to squint in the daylight.

"Well, that was quite a journey, my friend. Most intriguing but also quite enlightening. So tell me, in your own time, what comes to mind?"

"I don't know where to begin. I've never experienced anything even close to it. I was there! I felt like I was literally living in a different time—like a dream, but then so much more real."

"Does anything resonate with your past?"

"Not immediately. It was certainly not a time or place I've thought of before. Honestly, other than a slight interest in Chaucer's *Canterbury Tales* at school when I was studying for my O-Levels, I have not given a thought to that time."

"Have you ever read anything or watched a movie or play that might have prompted this?"

"Like I said, other than the *Canterbury Tales*, no."

"Most interesting. Tell me, have you heard of regression analysis?"

"Regression analysis? Other than as a part of my statistics class at school, no, never heard of it."

"Well, this is different. Let me give you a little background on regression analysis. It really started way back in the second century BC, when the Hindu scholar Patañjali, in his *Yoga Sutras*, discussed the idea of the soul becoming burdened with an accumulation of impressions as part of the karma from previous lives.

"Patañjali called the process of past-life regression *prati-prasav*, literally 'reverse birthing,' and saw it as addressing current problems through memories of past lives. Some types of yoga continue to use *prati-prasav* as a practice.

"Much later, a French educator named Allan Kardec—no relation to me by the way—also researched past life regression in *The Spirits Book* and *Heaven and Hell*.

"Past life regression therapy has been developed since the 1950s by psychologists, psychiatrists, and mediums. The belief gained credibility because some of the advocates possess legitimate credentials, though these credentials are in areas unrelated to religion, psychotherapy, or other domains dealing with past lives and mental health.

"Some practitioners use bridging techniques from a client's current-life problem to bring 'past-life stories' to conscious awareness. Practitioners believe that unresolved issues from alleged past lives may be the cause of their patients' problems.

"The memories are experienced as vivid as those based on events experienced in one's current life, impossible to differentiate from true memories of actual events from the present life, and accordingly, any damage can be difficult to undo.

"In essence, I believe you have just visualized and almost relived a past life experience!"

As I left Mr. Kardac's office and walked down the dimly lit staircase, I was suddenly taken aback by the realization that it was only a few hours before that I'd stepped up these same stairs, filled with anticipation and with a high level of apprehension.

Once in the car, I lit up a Dunhill, rolled down my driver-side window, and pulled out into the evening traffic heading south towards home. The sun was setting as I meandered through the streets of south Birmingham, wondering what might be going on in my fellow commuters' minds after mundane days in the office—a stark contrast to the thoughts flashing through my mind. I definitely needed a drink to reflect and relax.

Before I reached Edgbaston, I turned south on Harborne Road and pulled into the car park in front of The Physician, one of my all-time favorite pubs.

It took me a few minutes to find a quiet table in the corner away from the after-work throng. To reserve my spot, I left my car keys and cigarettes on the table and walked to the bar.

After a quick glance at the chalkboard, I ordered a steak and kidney pie with chips and a pint of Marston's Pedigree. Hard to find a decent pint in those days with the mighty breweries taking over and serving up cheap and nasty keg beer. But the smaller breweries were coming back and maintaining their focus on quality cask ale.

It was a nice, quiet dinner, giving me time to absorb and reflect. However, I remained quite confused by the supposed past life experience and could only think that I needed to return to learn more.

Once home, I ended my evening with an Ardbeg night cap and a cigarette before turning in for the night.

As I settled into bed, I couldn't help but think of the day's session with Mr. Kardac. What a day it had been!

Chapter Four

AS MY EYES OPENED, I WAS SURPRISED BY THE SUN SHINING through my bedroom window. I was that tired last night; I'd left the curtains wide open. Slipping out of bed, I realized I had slept a full night without waking and, even better, without nightmares. It was the first time in many months.

Walking towards the bay window, I glanced at my watch. I kept it on at night, as it was a self-winding one I'd bought long ago after I got tired of resetting one every morning. It was already 8:15 a.m. I couldn't believe it, as I'd usually wake before dawn, often in a cold sweat and feeling distraught. But on this morning, I was refreshed and relaxed.

Opening the bedroom windows, I looked down at the garden and was greeted by songbirds in full chorus.

"Coffee!" I said aloud.

Grabbing my dressing gown and slipping on my moccasins, I almost skipped down the stairs, feeling like a teenager. Once the kettle was on, I was ready for some music, something lively and cheerful. Vivaldi's *Four Seasons*. Perfect for my mood.

As the City of Birmingham Symphony Orchestra introduced "Spring," the kettle whistled. Fresh-ground Colombian would be just right. My cafetière filled, I took a coffee mug from the rack, opened the garden door handle with my knee, and strolled to my favorite garden chair.

"One more thing," I said.

Returning to the kitchen, I found my Dunhills on the counter, lighter next to them. Still half a pack left. I smiled and quickly returned to my seat.

Coffee and cigarettes: a magical combination. Healthy? Certainly not. But what a way to start the day.

The symphony orchestra moved on to the first bars of "Summer" as a bunch of crows launched into raucous squawking, hanging out like a gang of mobsters in the elm tree in my neighbor's garden.

Bliss.

I reflected on my previous day's visit with Mr. Kardac. I really didn't know what to make of it all but certainly felt something had shifted. Perhaps the hypnosis had broken a subconscious barrier? Who on earth was Owen, and where did that story come from? It was true that I'd enjoyed studying Chaucer at school, but that was mostly down to the fact that Jasper Cash my fifth-form teacher had a way of making it seem real and interesting. Anyway, the morning was too perfect to waste on mental analytics. What should I do with a whole Saturday ahead of me?

By the time the final chords of "Winter" faded away, my plan was made. A country drive and a pub lunch.

After a quick shower, I dressed in my old, faded Levi's and David Bowie T-shirt, grabbed my leather jacket, and hopped into the Jag.

Not being quite done with classical, I put Bruch's *Violin Concerto* on and pulled out of the driveway. Waving at Mrs. Hughes, my neighbor, off I went.

I took the A456 through Quintin and Hagley, passing by the Clent Hills. It was a glorious day with little traffic on the road.

I stopped at the newsagent's in Hagley and bought copies of *The Daily Mirror* and *The Guardian* and twenty Dunhills.

In under forty-five minutes I was backing into a parking space in front of the Queen's Head in Wolverley. The car park was quite empty for a Saturday morning: just a Land Rover, an MG GT, and an old-looking Morris Minor.

Once inside the bar, I picked a nice spot in the bay window, dropped my papers and cigarettes on the table, and turned towards the bar.

"Good morning, sir!"

"Good morning, indeed," I replied with a nod and a smile. "Pint of Banks's, if you please."

"Of course, sir. Straight or handle?"

"Straight of course!"

"Well, I always 'as to ask, sir. We gets quite a few hoity-toities at the Queen's these days. That'll be 50p, thank you, sir."

"Well, at least the prices haven't gone up yet."

"Next week, wouldn't you know it. They'm upping 'em 10p a pint."

"Such is progress!" I laughed and settled down in my seat to peruse my newspapers.

The reading was none to cheery. Norton Triumph motor-cycles going into liquidation. Another bakers' strike. Gun spree in West Bromwich with four killed. Turning to the back pages: it's Monza tomorrow. Mario Andretti is on pole.

"I love Formula One racing; there is nothing quite so exciting and yet so dangerous," I said out loud.

"Aye, that's what makes it, sir," the bartender replied. "Will be interesting to see how Hunt the Shunt and Niki do. They're a fine pair they are! I loves our James. Out gallivant-ing all night with the ladies and then 'e 'ops in 'is McClaren and off 'e goes like a rocket. Never known anyone like 'im!"

"Well, Andretti is going to be hard to beat, and he's already got the championship just about locked up."

"You never know?"

Engrossed in *The Guardian*, I hardly noticed a new customer at the bar.

"The usual, Robert?" the Barman asked.

"You know it!"

I glance up over my paper to see a tall young man with long flowing golden locks and dressed in a faded denim shirt, skin-tight leather trousers, and high-heeled snakeskin boots.

Pint in hand, he turned and raised his glass towards me.

"Cheers! Lovely day our kid."

Slight Black Country accent and a broad grin. It was Robert Plant!

"Lovely indeed. I drove over from Birmingham, and it couldn't have been lovelier."

"That your Jag out front?"

"Yes. I love that car."

"And well you should; it's a beauty. Mind if I join you?"

"I'd be honored."

"Hah! Did you hear that, Bill? He obviously don't know who I am!"

"Robert Plant of Led Zep?!"

"You got me there. But here in the Queen's I'm simply Robert. Pleased to meet you."

As he reached out his hand, I clasped it tightly and introduced myself.

With respect, I deliberately avoided the usual clichéd questions about the wild Led Zeppelin days, though in truth I was sorely tempted. We mostly talked about the current state of football; he being a Wolves fan and I a Baggies fan, there was mutual respect. Then we got into a long conversation about mysticism and the ancient Celtic culture. I was impressed with his knowledge and original perspectives and could see where many of the band's songs originated. When I shared my story of my hypnotism, he was engrossed.

"There's more to this world than we simple mortals will ever know," he said.

"Sounds like a lyric in the making!" I retorted.

"Might be at that!" he said with a laugh.

After three pints, it was time for both of us to get moving. I had a drive ahead of me, and he had the grass to cut. Only a few miles from the pub, his country house was set on ten acres of grass that were in dire need of cutting, he said with a grin.

"Nothing beats the land, you know. That and a good woman."

"I'm with you on the land, but I've yet to find the right woman."

"Patience maketh the man! Lovely meeting you. Come back to our local soon."

He handed his empty glass to the barman and was out the door in a flash. I looked out the window to see him get into a muddy Range Rover and race off down the country lane.

Driving home, I was feeling quite elated. Perhaps the beer helped, but I felt like something magical was happening to me. The hypnosis had definitely opened up my subconscious, but then I meet Robert Plant and talk about mysticism: was that just a coincidence?

Led Zeppelin I blasted out as I drove home. "Dazed and Confused." That captured how I felt, though not related to a woman but to my life.

After stopping at the fish and chip shop on the High Street in Edgbaston, I was all set for the night. I watched *Dr. Who* at 5 p.m., *The Two Ronnies* later, and then wrapped it up with Match of the Day.

I was in bed a little after 11 p.m. and slept like a baby.

Sunday's were generally my "day of rest." Not being a churchgoer, I would usually enjoy a leisurely full English breakfast with a pot of Lapsang souchong tea, followed by a day of reading and relaxation. However, that Sunday was the Italian Grand Prix at Monza and that was something I didn't want to miss.

So, after finishing my breakfast, which included a nice few slices of black pudding from "James the Butchers," I did the washing up and switched on the television.

The BBC was televising the race live, largely due to the continued popularity of James Hunt and his ongoing duel with Niki Lauda. That year, though, they'd both been pipped by Mario Andretti, who was pretty much indomitable.

I poured myself another cup of tea and waited for the start.

Andretti took pole position alongside Gilles Villeneuve (Ferrari), with Jean-Pierre Jabouille (Renault) in third place, Lauda in fourth, and Peterson in fifth.

The race starter was overenthusiastic, turning on the red lights before all the cars had lined up; several cars in the middle of the field got a jump on those at the front. The result was a funneling effect of the cars approaching the chicane, and the cars were tightly bunched together with little room to maneuver. James Hunt was overtaken on the right-hand side by Riccardo Patrese, and Hunt instinctively veered left and hit the rear right wheel of Peterson's Lotus 78, with Vittorio Brambilla, Hans-Joachim Stuck, Patrick Depailler, Didier Pironi, Derek Daly, Clay Regazzoni, and Brett Lunger all involved in the ensuing melee.

Peterson's Lotus went into the barriers hard on the right-hand side and caught fire. He was trapped, but Hunt, Regazzoni, and Depailler managed to free him from the wreck before he received more than minor burns. He was dragged free and laid in the middle of the track fully conscious, but with severe leg injuries. It took twenty minutes before medical help arrived at the scene. Brambilla—who had been hit on the head by a flying wheel and rendered unconscious—and Peterson were taken to the Niguarda hospital in nearby Milan.

The race was restarted nearly three hours later, during which time on the formation lap for the second race, Jody Scheckter's Wolf lost a wheel and crashed at the second Lesmo curve, bending the Armco barrier that was situated right next to the track.

Andretti, Hunt, Lauda, Carlos Reutemann, and Emerson Fittipaldi all went to the spot where Scheckter crashed, and upon inspection of the state of the barrier, they refused to start until it was repaired, causing more delay. Because of the amount of time between the first and second races, the distance was shortened to forty laps. The second start was at nearly 6:00 p.m.

Villeneuve overtook Andretti at the restart, but both drivers were judged to have gone early and given a one-minute penalty. Lauda finished ahead of John Watson (Brabham), Carlos Reutemann (Ferrari), Jacques Laffite (Ligier-Matra), and Patrick Tambay (McLaren-Ford).

Andretti and Villeneuve were dropped to sixth and seventh places. Andretti had won the championship, but with Peterson in hospital, celebrations were muted.

For the rest of the day, I stayed indoors, as the weather had turned quite chilly, and a typical English drizzle had settled in. Daphne du Maurier's *House on the Strand* kept me fully engrossed until early evening, by which time I was getting hungry. Not having much that I fancied in the fridge, I popped out to The Bombay House around the corner and ordered a chicken korma, garlic naan, and rice takeaway.

Back home, I watched an old episode of *Last of the Summer Wine* with my curry on a tray. A fitting way to end a perfect weekend.

On Monday morning I was up at the crack of dawn, showered, and dressed in my new blue silk and wool three-piece suit in preparation for a morning meeting in Redditch.

My major project over the prior six weeks had been a design for a new mixed-purpose community to be located on the outskirts of Redditch. The urban sprawl of Birmingham during the early 1970s had just about turned Redditch into a commuter town. The city's historical character and charm had been consumed by concrete shopping centers and cookie-cutter housing estates. A visionary mayor had been elected the prior year and immediately devised a plan to manage the growth, maintain what was remaining of the character, and create a blueprint for future development intended to recreate the communal feel that the city had lost.

My proposed design was a late twentieth century adaptation of the concepts incorporated into the Cadbury brothers' remarkable creation of Bournville. Built on open space a few miles southeast of Birmingham during the late 1800s, Bournville was radical. The Cadbury brothers' goal was to provide a quality living environment for their chocolate factory workers, including schools, parks, shops, and entertainment facilities set in amongst well-architected dwellings. It was a far cry from the slums of most English industrial towns. It had been a tremendous success and fostered many other so-called model towns spread around England.

Although the Redditch Project was not of the same scale of Bournville, it did offer an opportunity to accomplish something special and unique.

Monday morning traffic was light heading down the A441. As I passed by the signs for Bournville on my right, I felt my confidence grow. Arriving at the Redditch Town Hall almost half an hour early, I parked the car and walked across the road to a small tea shop for a cup of tea and a bacon sandwich.

The meeting began promptly at 8 a.m. with the mayor's introduction. The town council members were all present, at least physically, though most of them gave the appearance of preferring to be anywhere but where they were. More interested in the tea and biscuits than their mayor's speech.

Having made many presentations to hostile or at least disinterested groups during my career, I was quite prepared to stir them up by appealing to their egos.

"Thank you, Mr. Mayor. Thank you, honorable Council Members. I am sincerely both appreciative and thrilled at the opportunity to meet with you today. We have before us the unique opportunity to build a legacy the like of which has never before been accomplished. A legacy that will be the envy of towns and cities all across England."

The tea cups were set down, the biscuit plates pushed aside, and I now had their full attention.

After an hour of showing designs on the overhead projector, I concluded the meeting with my closing statement.

"Today's meeting can go down in history as the beginning of the Redditch renewal—the creation of a community the like of which has never been seen before. I put it to you to be the Council Members who made this happen!"

Done.

Picking up my papers and folders, I left the conference room to wait outside while they deliberated.

The mayor's secretary was nice enough to fetch me a cup of tea from the cafeteria while I sat reflecting on the meeting.

A mere fifteen minutes passed before the mayor stormed out with a broad grin on his face.

"Well, young man, you've done it! You better be true to your word because you have created a level of excitement and a very high expectation from a group I normally struggle to keep awake. Well done, indeed."

Shaking his hand, I could hardly contain my joy. Thus was a momentous achievement.

My drive home was nothing short of delightful. In honor of John Bonham (Led Zeppelin drummer) who was born in Redditch, I listened to *Led Zeppelin 4*. Bonzo's drumming on "When the Levee Breaks" was nothing short of amazing. Then, for a more peaceful ambience, I put Bruch's *Scottish Fantasy* in the eight-track. It was perfect for the occasion and reminded me that I'd been planning to make an attempt at cooking haggis. Perhaps a good celebration with a bottle of Spanish Rioja? Yes. As I already had the recipe stored in my memory, I turned off towards Sainsbury's to purchase my ingredients.

By a little past six o'clock, I was in the kitchen experimenting with my Scottish delicacy whilst sipping a nice glass of wine. As a tribute to Scotland, I put on Gerry Rafferty's Stealers Wheel.

Tomorrow evening I would be returning to Mr. Kardac for my next session. I wondered what that would have in store for me? But for the present, I was immersed in my haggis.

Chapter Five

ORLANDO PRYCE

(1586-1666)

WITHIN A FEW MINUTES OF SITTING IN KARDAC'S THERAPY chair, I was in a different place, in the past again.

Angelic a cappella voices drift through the towering medieval arches of Worcester Cathedral where I find myself once again.

Today, however, I am not in the front pews where the choristers sit, but looking over their shoulders in the lay clerk's pew behind them. Dressed in crisp white surplice over a deep scarlet robe and with a starched ruffle tightly wrapped around my neck, I am in the throes of the "Agnus Dei" by William Byrd. A truly breathtaking piece in four parts. As the final harmonies fade into the arches of the nave, we sit for the closing prayers of Holy Communion.

The timelessness of the music and the setting make it hard to tell when this is taking place, until I glance around the congregation seated in stalls all around me. They are dressed mostly in black as is appropriate for Sunday Holy Communion; however, the men are wearing doublet and hose, and the women, ankle-length dresses with fine lace collars. I must be somewhere in the sixteenth century, I think.

After the service, we are in the chapter house, another familiar place for me, changing from our vestments into our Sunday clothes. Mine are hanging on a peg with my name above written in ink on a parchment card, "O. Pryce."

"Coming down the Cardinal's for a beer, Orlando?"

I turn to face a tall, skinny man with bright red hair hanging down to his shoulders and dressed in his Sunday finery. No black for Charlie; he's decked out in a purple jacket with shiny silver buttons, a white neckerchief, and bright red hose. As he adjusts his leather belt, he flashes a grin at me.

"Or did you have a few too many jars yesternight? A 'hair of the dog' would do the trick, I should say, Orlando."

The Cardinal's Hat is just a few minutes' walk from the cathedral along Friar Street. In my days living in Worcester, New Street appeared anything but new; lines of black-and-white Elizabethan houses leaned over the street, almost as if they were swaying towards one another. This day, they appear brand new and freshly painted, with not a sway in sight! The Cardinal's Hat I knew was a mostly Victorian structure; this, the original pub, is a black-and-white oak-beamed house. The bar inside is snug and warm and already crowded with noon Sunday drinkers, almost all men. I suppose in these days it is inappropriate for women to be seen in pubs, else they will gain a reputation; the only two women in the bar are the barmaid and a gaudily dressed young woman unashamedly plying her trade.

Charlie is immediately engrossed in conversation with her, leaning and leering intently.

I meanwhile am content with my ale; that is, until I notice the oddly dressed gentleman seated in the bay window. I am intrigued by his demeanor. He exudes a worldliness, or is it an unworldliness? I am perplexed. He is staring straight at me.

"Orlando Pryce, would you do me the honor of allowing me to buy you a beverage?"

"Sir, you do me a disservice, for I know not who you are! I am fully familiar with societal etiquette, as I was well educated at the King's School."

"Verily, you were indeed, and have become an exemplary member of the finest choir in England."

"That, sir, is debatable! However, you still have me at your advantage."

"May I introduce myself as Bernael, Bernael Le Ciffre. Honored to finally make your acquaintance."

"How do you know of me?"

"You have been under my watchful eye for some time, Mr. Pryce. I am, sir, a sincere advocate of your career, and highly impressed with your recent compositions."

"My recent compositions?"

"Your eight-part *Sanctae Crucis* was impeccable and in my humble opinion surpassed even Tallis's *Spem in Alium*."

"Really? No, you are playing me the fool!"

"In truth, it was sublime. You are vastly underrated and held back by the insecurity and lack of talent of Mr. Tompkins."

"Thomas? Our king, god bless him though he be a Scot, would disagree. Despite his passion for purging the Catholics since the Guy Fawkes incident, he still remains an ardent advocate of the fine arts. This past year he named him Gentleman Extraordinary in the Chapel Royal no less. He's the best musician in the land."

"Your talent will surpass, if only you are given the opportunity. Come bide with me, Orlando Pryce, that I might henceforth share a proposition for your consideration."

"How's about that drink you offered? Another ale if you please."

"Our meeting and our conversation deserve the very best French brandy and nothing less."

"Betty! Two of your best brandies, in clean glasses, mind you! We'll be seated over yon."

Now seated in the window, Bernael begins.

"As I said, I have taken a keen interest in your career, Orlando, and have it in my power to enable you to become the greatest composer in the land, and with it, deserved fame and fortune."

"What are you, then? A music publisher? In truth, you dress unlike any I've acquainted."

"I am merely an interested party with influence. Should you compose six pieces for me in the coming year, I will guarantee their success."

"How on earth in God's name can you promise such a thing?"

"Not in His name, but in my lord's name. He will grant this for you if you grant him his wish."

"What be that, then?"

"Your soul, Mr. Pryce. He will grant you fame and fortune in this life for your soul in another life."

"Hah! I may have sung in a cathedral for nigh on twenty years now, but I ain't no religious man. That be for the wealthy and pious, in my book. Neither of which be I! There be only one life, and assuredly that be enough for me."

The brandy is warming my innards, and the proposition is warming my heart. I am not taking it all very seriously, but then what's to lose?

"And what if I don't become famous? What then?"

"You will, I can assure you, become very famous, but as you clearly have doubt, in answer to your question, the agreement would become void and you would keep your soul."

"Then, I say, let's drink to it!" I raise my glass with a broad grin.

"A small matter, but I will need your signature on this document if you please."

He reaches into his inside jacket pocket and removes a rolled parchment with a black ribbon. From his other pocket appears a quill pen and small silver ink pot.

"You come prepared, Mr. Le Ciffre! How could you know I'd agree?"

"I've known you these thirty years, through school and choir. I know you well, Orlando Pryce."

Having signed my name, I step away for a leak, only to return and find him gone.

"Where did he go, Betty?"

"Who, love?"

"The fancy-dressed gentlemen I was sitting with."

"Oh! I don't recall. Must have left, I suppose."

I finish my brandy in silence, mulling over what just transpired. Must be a joke, for sure. Yes, just a joke.

My vision fades but then adjusts and I'm seated in the same spot but now in a small group chatting convivially. Each appears well dressed in finery as they sip glasses of wine.

"Might be the last wine we enjoy for some time, so let us make the most."

"Aye! Oliver's army is well settled in over at St. John's ward, and they ain't budging. I'm sick and tired of the daily barrages. Feels to me like we are mere sitting ducks."

"Well, John, I've been saying for some time now that we must attack. Best line of defense is offense! No point hauling up and hoping for reprieve 'cos it ain't coming. Prince Rupert was our last hope and he's now refurbishing in Oxford. We must harass the roundheads!"

"I'm with you, Henry Townsend!" I hear my own voice joining in the debate.

"I know you're of a like mind, Orlando, but pardon my directness: we need soldiers not singers."

"No offense taken, Henry. You're completely correct. Hardly likely to see me wielding a sword! More like a songbook!"

"Aye, Orlando, but your sweet music lifts our spirits, which at a time like this is worth its weight in gold. This siege has been intolerable, and folks are losing heart and getting downright distraught. 'Tis four years we've been suffering this civil war, and there's no end in sight 'cepting a Protestant victory."

I look around and the Cardinal's Hat is filled to the brim. Spirits seem high to me, despite Henry's foreboding.

"One more round, then I'm off to night watch…"

The bar fades away again, and I feel I'm drifting then resurfacing slowly into another place.

I'm conducting. The choir is before me. All eyes are on me. Heavenly sounds echo through the arches. I am again in Worcester Cathedral, but now leading the choir in what sounds ethereal though intricately complex, the harmonies and counterpoints unlike any I've heard. As the angelic voices fade, I am taken aback as the congregation stands and claps. This is unheard of; nobody claps in a church.

I look around me and cannot believe my eyes. Standing and applauding passionately is my namesake, Orlando Gibbons, and then beside him, Thomas Morley—the two greatest composers in England. There across the aisle stands Thomas Tallis with hand on heart as he rests on his cane. I, Orlando Pryce, born of humble means in St. John's ward of Worcester, am being honored and praised by the greatest composers of my generation!

It all fades quickly, and I am now once more seated in the bar of the Cardinal's Hat.

"Thank heavens that crusty old fart Oliver is gone. Good riddance. Handsome Charles is now our king. He knows how to enjoy life, and I'll love him for it! Have another brandy, love? You look like you need one. Seen a ghost?"

I look up and see Betty, now old and grey, looking towards me. My hands are wrinkled, and as I touch my cheeks, I feel deep crevices.

"Is my name Orlando or what?"

"Always the joker! There you go, lover."

She reaches down and places the glass before me, then leans forward across the table and kisses my cheek.

"You're a sweetheart, Orlando. Bin a good customer and a good friend too these many long years. Despite your fame and fortune you always was a loyal one. God bless you."

I realize that the years have passed, and I'm back where I started, or at least where I met Le Ciffre. Whoever he was, I'll never know, but his prophecies came true. I have indeed become the greatest composer in England. I have lived a life of fame and fortune. I have met kings and queens and traveled across Europe, conducting my music to constant accolades. It all came true. But now what? What is next?

As I look around the bar, the familiar faces are smiling. My friends and companions these many years all gathered in my favorite place. Then I pick out Bernael Le Ciffre standing by the bar, looking towards me and beckoning me.

"It is time. It is time, Orlando."

The room becomes bleary. The smiling faces turn to demonic grins. I feel I am slipping down in my seat. I look down and the tiles turn to a mass of writhing arms and legs, bodies twisted in torment, hands reach up to me and grab at my legs, dragging me down and down. I see Le Ciffre nodding.

If you've ever fainted, you know how it felt as I came back. It truly felt like I was struggling to return, almost clawing my way back to reality. Blackness turned to grey, then a tunnel of vision appeared and slowly opened up as I saw Kardac leaning over me and the room reappearing.

"Are you doing okay, James?" I heard his voice, but it sounded like it was coming through a distant speaker.

At first, I couldn't form words, then I heard myself speaking. "Uh! I think so. That was intense!"

"Well naturally, James, it would be very intense, as you've just experienced another past life. What it means, we will have to explore. But for now just relax and breathe deeply and slowly."

"When you're ready, tell me how you feel and what resonates with you."

I tried to collect my thoughts and reflect.

"It was so real, like I was actually there. More than a dream, it was as if it were truly happening to me."

"Well, perhaps it did. But it's important that you tell me what meant something to you, before it fades back into your subconscious."

"The Cardinal's Hat keeps coming back and the cathedral and the choir. Then Orlando Pryce; that was the name on the tomb in the cathedral that came back to me earlier. I've never heard of him, but now I feel like I know him."

"Yes indeed, you have a strong connection to those places and to Orlando. Just as you had a connection to Owen. It is all about the connections. As we uncover those, we will uproot the cause of your nightmares."

"I suppose."

"There is no suppose. This is reality, and I can guarantee that once we find the root of your subconscious fear, we will release it. But for now, you've had a very exhausting experience and should go home and rest. We can continue in a few days."

As I drove home, I wondered if this was a "chicken or egg." Was my mind creating these stories based upon my past experiences, or did they really happen and remain in my subconscious? I wasn't sure which explanation I preferred.

That evening, once home, I put on Pink Floyd's "Echoes," poured a healthy measure of Ardbeg, and slumped down on the couch with a cigarette. It was all too much to process.

I awoke on the couch and, glancing over at the clock, saw that it was past midnight.

Chapter Six

⸺⸙⸺

THE FOLLOWING SATURDAY I DECIDED I'D CELEBRATE MY Redditch success with a day of music and football.

Still in my pajamas and dressing gown, I kicked it off with "John Barleycorn Must Die" by Traffic, opened wide my French doors to the patio, and settled into my favorite garden chair. Colombian coffee and cigarettes by my side, I looked out at the plethora of colors in the garden while the sun peaked through the clouds. It was quite perfect. Winwood working his magic on "Empty Pages" brought tears of joy to my eyes. Life doesn't get better than this, I thought. How different I felt after just two sessions with Kardac. I hoped he might help me with my nightmares but never imagined he would open up a whole new world to me. Maybe a past world, but somehow it was real and connected me to a past—whether my past or someone else's didn't seem to really matter.

My neighbor was now mowing his lawn, which normally would have intruded and irritated me, but today I simply cranked up the volume on the stereo and settled back into my bliss.

I'd started my music day with Traffic as they were truly a local band. Stevie Winwood grew up in Handsworth, a stone's throw from me; Chris Wood was from Quinton; Jim Capaldi, Evesham; and Dave Mason from where I was born in Worcester. I felt a strong connection to them. As a kid I remember walking to school past Mason's Newsagents Shop across from All Saints Church, not knowing at the time that it was Dave Mason's dad's. My first singles that I bought included "Paper Sun" and "Hole in My Shoe." Along with my collection of Beatles and Stones forty-fives, I sold them all for a pittance to Swindling Harry, who owned the secondhand shop around the corner. Should have kept them, as they'd have been worth a mint one day, but instead I spent the money on fags. Oh well!

Finishing my coffee, I went in for a refresh and switched the music to ELO, the Electric Light Orchestra. Courtesy of Roy Wood and Jeff Lynne, a whole new genre of music had been invented in 1970. Bands had dabbled at incorporating a classical influence, but ELO totally integrated it.

"10538 Overture" had been a top-ten hit in 1971. I remembered that the album the song was on was released in the States as *No Answer* because when the record company secretary called the UK company, nobody answered the phone, so they named it "No Answer." Funny story, I thought. I was sticking with my local theme: Roy was from Kitts Green and Jeff grew up in Erdington on the north side of Birmingham.

For my third and final cup of coffee, I switched over to the Moody Blues; yet another Birmingham band, though a lot older. They had started up in Erdington in 1964. They got their name because Mike Pinder was interested in how music changes people's moods and due to the fact that the band was playing blues at the time. Around this time, the band was the resident group at the Carlton Ballroom, later to become rock music venue Mothers on Erdington High Street. But then after financial misfortune and a confrontation with an audience member, the band soon realized that their style of American blues covers and novelty tunes was not working and decided to perform primarily their own material. Their Deram record label executives were initially skeptical about the hybrid style of the resulting concept album, *Days of Future Passed*, released in November 1967, but it peaked at number twenty-seven on the British LP chart. Five years later, it reached number three on the *Billboard* chart in the US. The LP was one of the first concept albums that takes place over the course of a single day. The album drew inspiration in production and arrangement from the pioneering use of classical instrumentation by the Beatles, to whom Pinder had introduced the mellotron that year. It took the form to new heights using the London Festival Orchestra, a loose affiliation of Decca's classical musicians given a fictitious name, adding the word "London" to sound impressive. The orchestra provided a linking framework to the Moodies' already written and performed songs, plus overture and conclusion sections on the album, including backing up Graeme Edge's opening and closing poems recited by Pinder. Strings were added to the latter portion of the album version of Justin Hayward's "Nights in White Satin" (absent on the single), but the orchestra and group never performed together on the recording, with the band's rock instrumentation centered on Pinder's mellotron. Despite being a lush concept album, the LP was cut in a very workmanlike manner, with the band recording a particular song, then the track being presented to Peter Knight, their producer, who quickly composed a suitable "linking" orchestral portion that the Decca musicians (London Festival Orchestra) then recorded. The album was as much an original work by Knight himself as the group. Sorry, going on a bit there, but I'm a bit of a music nut!

And so I listened to the *Days of Future Passed* as I finished off my coffee.

After a nice, warm shower, I got dressed in jeans and a sweat-shirt, put on my leather jacket, and wrapped my blue-and-white

West Brom scarf round my neck, before heading out the front door; no way was I repeating the Tottenham fracas.

I'd decided on a late pub breakfast of steak and kidney pie, chips, and a pint on my way to the West Brom game. With lots of time on hand, I enjoyed a leisurely lunch in the Cross Keys on the outskirts of the city center. I thought I'd avoid the football crowds, and I was right—I had the pub almost to myself.

It was a smashing game! The Baggies were in fine form and utterly demolished Manchester United by a final score of five to three. Tony "Bomber" Brown scored two with typically mighty shots; Cyrille and Laurie both scored with Len Cantello adding the fifth.

What a day it was turning out to be! And I still had the evening in store: night clubbing at the Rum Runner. Although it wasn't the most healthy thing to do, I thoroughly enjoyed two hot dogs smothered in fried onions outside the club before I lined up and went in.

The Rum Runner was a pretty seedy joint. Low ceilings except for the stage area, which itself was quite small. But that created an intimacy just right for up-and-coming bands; you almost felt like you were listening to them playing in their living room. I sat down at the bar and ordered a lager, no decent beer being available. Carling Black Label, a sorry attempt at lager, but there you have it.

The crowd was starting to pour in, and I deliberated over moving closer to the stage, but decided that the ability to order a drink at ease trumped proximity to the music, which likely would be deafening anyway.

A new local band by the name of Duran Duran was on that night. Nobody had heard of them.

"So, who's this band on tonight?" I asked the barman.

"Local lads. Duran Duran they calls 'emselves. Mack was saying they cum in a few weeks back with a demo tape, and he offered them a gig if they'd work around the club. Turns out they might be best sticking to working in the club to my mind."

"What's the music like?"

"Bit affected for my taste, synthesizers and all that shit, you know, but then I'm a Hawkwind fan."

"Way of the future, so they say. Lead guitarists becoming dinosaurs, but we will have to see."

"But they're nice lads. Roger, the drummer, cleans glasses; Andy cooks a bit and cleans up; John works the door some nights, bouncer like; and the other one, Nick, I think, is not a bad DJ."

As it turned out, it was not the most memorable of nights. They had trouble with their sound system and looked like they were more into their looks than their music. But having said that, they did have something. Definitely needed a good lead singer.

What I liked though, was that they were trying something new, going in a different direction. To me that was what it was all about.

Earlier that year I'd seen The Clash at Barbarella's in May, Dire Straits in July, and the Sex Pistols just a couple of months ago. Each very different with a lot to say. I liked that. I liked Barbarella's too, as they always had good bands.

The set was quite short, and after a couple more nasty lagers, I ducked out for a decent pint of Marston's at The Physician on my way home to Edgbaston.

It was a lovely day indeed. Tomorrow, I thought I'd head down to Worcester for the day. Might be good to see how I felt there after my experiences with the past, each centered around

Worcester, plus it would be nice to revisit the Cardinal's Hat after many years and perhaps pay my respects to the cathedral.

So, Sunday morning, after an uninterrupted night's sleep and after a cup of coffee with a couple of slices of peanut butter on toast, I got on the road to head home towards my birthplace.

Sunday morning traffic was understandably light on the M5, allowing me to drive down the London Road into the city center just before opening time. Parking right outside the Cardinal's on New Street, I had a few minutes to stand under the cover of the baker's shop next door, avoiding the slight drizzle while enjoying a Dunhill before the doors opened.

Promptly at twelve, I heard the key turning in the lock and didn't wait to be the first into the bar. As I walked in, I looked around, feeling like I was back home. It had been a good ten years since I had been here, but it felt like yesterday. The dark oak panels and low-beamed ceiling made a cozy, welcoming atmosphere.

It seemed like nothing had changed, and I was pleased to find the Davenports handles lined along the bar.

"Good morning, young sir. Eager for a beer I'd take it?"

"Verily. A pint of your best bitter would suffice."

I heard myself talking in a medieval accent. Odd!

"Whereabouts you from then, sir?"

"Well, I was born in Ronkswood, grew up in St. John's, went to the King's School, then ended up in Birmingham."

"Sorry about that, sir."

"Sorry?"

"Brumigem! Who'd want to live there?"

"Oh! It's not that bad. Has its good side when you get used to it, but I do have to say I miss the peace and quiet of Worcester."

"Peace and quiet? Dead as the grave more like, I'd say!"

"Hah!"

"King's boy, eh? How was that?"

"Painful. Though it set me in good stead."

"Used to get a lot of them teachers down here, but seems like these days they prefer the White Hart. Closer to home I suppose."

A few couples started to come into the bar, and preferring my peace and quiet, I moved into the lounge behind the bar. It was just as always: big old stone fireplace and paneled walls. I'd forgotten the framed prints on the walls and took the time to study them. Worcester in the late Middle Ages—that somehow felt quite familiar.

After two pints, I was ready for a breath of fresh air and a walk, so I bid my farewell to the bartender and headed off towards the cathedral. It all came back as I sat on a bench in the cathedral gardens overlooking the River Severn. I felt like I was returned to my choir days, or was I returned to Orlando's days?

I decided to take a walk and continue my nostalgia, wondering if it would bring some clarity. Walking down the steps through the water gate and under the trees along the riverbank, I turned up Severn Street. Passing the "New Block" built in the early seventies long after I'd left school, I couldn't help but critique the design through my architect's eyes. Quite incongruous and out of place amongst mostly early Victorian structures. Another example of function over form.

As I passed through the school gardens, the memories flooded back. My school years were not exactly the most enjoyable of times, and my mood was taken over by long-past emotions of worry and stress.

Quite relieved to arrive in the grass circle leading up to the cathedral, I walked under the ancient archway, through which I had passed many a time on my way to choir practice.

The musty smell of old stone immediately hit me, and just as our sense of smell takes us back, I could have been eight years of age, entering these sacred cloisters for the first time. The chapter house, where Orlando conducted choir practice, was deserted. I sat on the bench as I had thousands of times in my youth and looked down at the carvings in the wooden music stand. I found my initials "JP" deeply etched in capital letters.

Glancing at my watch, I realized it was already 4:00 p.m. as I heard the cathedral organ in the distance. I was in the mood to listen to the Sunday Evensong.

As the service had commenced, I quietly took a seat in the back and reviewed the Order of Service leaflet. It included "O Vos Omnes," composed by one of the altos, and "Magnificat" by Christopher Robinson, the current choirmaster. Both very modern and quite discordant; I was not too impressed. However, the choir was magnificent, and I was glad that I attended.

After the service, I strolled through the nave and stopped at Orlando's tomb. Touching it, I felt a slight shiver run up my spine and took my hand away abruptly.

"What is the connection?" I said to myself.

But I'd had enough for one day and briskly walked to my car parked outside the Cardinal's and headed home to Edgbaston.

The weekend had left me with more questions than answers.

Chapter Seven

JACK PRICE

(1721–1781)

AFTER MY TRIP TO WORCESTER OVER THE WEEKEND, I FELT a mixture of confusion and curiosity, but also a certain level of excitement. I wanted to find out more. What could be behind all of this? How did any of it relate to my life? Would Kardac really be able to relieve my nightmares?

I had many questions and was eager to bring some clarity to my situation.

So, when it came time for my next appointment with Kardac, I was really quite intrigued and receptive to learning more.

It was Thursday evening, and I was seated comfortably, fully relaxed and attentive, as he prepared me for my third exploration. It was only moments before I shifted into the past.

It seems as though I am awaking from a dream as my immediate surroundings slowly come into focus. Before me is a pewter mug sitting on a well-worn heavy wooden table covered in scratches and stains. My hands are resting on the edge of the table in front of me. As I stare down at them, they appear rough and stained, my fingernails ragged and crusted with dirt. I lift them close to my face and sniff. I can smell hops.

As I look up and my eyes adjust, I can tell I am sitting in what reminds me of an old English pub: dark wood beams across a low ceiling, wooden tables around a cozy room with burning candles giving a low glow to the scene, and a bar to my left.

I am seated in a bay window with heavy curtains drawn closed. Where am I? I draw the curtains apart, crane my neck, and glimpse a coach and horses passing by on a narrow road. Looking up to my left, I can just make out the sign swinging in the breeze; it reads "The Fox Inn."

I reach into my trouser pocket in the hope of discovering more about who I am. I pull out a scrap of paper and spread it open on the table.

"Godfrey Winwood, Merchant, The Hop Market, Worcester. Thirty-six bushels Bransford Hops twenty-one shillings and thruppence farthing paid in full." It is a crumpled receipt.

"How's the 'arvest, Jack?"

I am startled and look up to see the barman wiping the counter and looking directly at me. I must be Jack. Without hesitation, I hear myself replying in a voice and heavy accent I cannot recognize.

"Don't ask me, Will. I've took three wagonloads to the 'op market in Worcester this past week and 'ardly made enough to make it through the winter, let alone to next 'arvest!"

"Aye, I know times is tough for you small holdings. Them big landowners is driving down the prices. And the breweries are paying jack shit."

"Tell me about it, Will! I can 'ardly afford a beer anymore."

"I hears Meg's place is up for sale. Nice bit a' land there, I'd say."

"Right, I heard that too. Love to get my 'ands on that place! Cost a fair penny, I'm sure. I'm cursed being in the shadow of Bramley Wood and 'ardly catch a bit of sun. Me 'ops struggle to even reach the lines!"

"Ah! 'Tis a hard lot, Jack Price."

I gulp a good swig of my beer and wipe my lips, repeating to myself, "Yeah, I'd love to get my 'ands on Meg's place, but there's no way."

"There is a way."

"What was that?"

"There is a way."

"Beg pardon, but I couldn't help but overhear your conversation. Perchance I can be of assistance if you will allow me. May I join you?"

Without awaiting my response, he stands up from his table. His appearance is unlike anything I've ever seen before. He is dressed in doublet and hose, his jacket adorned with jeweled buttons, and he is wearing a wide-brimmed felt hat casting a shadow over his face. As he comes closer, I can more clearly make out his facial features: dark, almost black, eyes with a piercing nature, distinctive and prominent nose, wide mouth and thin lips with a firmness about them that convey resolve, and long black hair falling from beneath his hat to his shoulders. A jewel that looks like a ruby dangles from his left ear. His look is unworldly, almost alien, as if he is from another time. I am mesmerized for a few seconds and then gather my thoughts to ask, "Where you from then? I can't place your accent, and as for your dress, it baffles me!"

"Ah! All over. My work takes me wherever I'm needed, and my dress is to my liking."

That was no response, but I let it go.

"May I introduce myself: I am Bernael Le Ciffre, originally a French name, I believe. Jack, may I call you by your first name?"

"Bin called a lot worse."

"Jack, I have a proposition for you."

"What be that then?"

"An advance, in return for something from you."

"Ooh! 'Ark at them there fancy words! What be an advance when he's at 'ome?"

"Sufficient gold to purchase Meg's farm outright."

"It be an 'opyard; ain't no farm."

"I stand corrected, but nevertheless my proposition is on the table."

"What's in it for you? What do you get in return?"

"Your soul."

"My soul? What on earth would you do with my soul?"

"Jack, that's for me to worry about. That's my business: collecting souls."

"Struth! Sounds like a deal to me. What do I need with a soul anyway?"

"Don't you believe in the afterlife, Jack?"

"Ain't got no time for thinking 'bout no afterlife; this one's hard enough for me. Nor do I have time for that churchgoing twaddle. All the while them there churchgoers is resting on their arses on them there pews, I be up to me arms in me 'ops pruning and the like. No, ain't got no time for that horse shit. What's the church ever done for me?"

"I hear you, Jack. I'm of a similar view regarding the church. The person I work for delivers in this life. No need to wait for the next life."

"I'll drink to that."

"How about another one, Jack? Same again or maybe something stronger? A whiskey, perhaps?"

"Don't mind if I do."

I watch as he walks to the bar, wondering what just happened. Could it be possible that I could get Meg's hopyard? That would surely be a miracle. I'd get three times the hops or even more. And the best hops at that. What's to lose?

He sets the glass down in front of me and smiles. "Cheers, Jack! I have a feeling that this may be the best decision you've ever made."

"Ain't made no decision yet, but I'm pondering it."

"Well then, why not sleep on it? We can meet again tomorrow to tell me your decision."

"Right you are then."

That night I am restless and keep waking with a start. However I try, I cannot get the stranger I recently met out of my mind—it is as if he is still here with me. I see his wide lips turning into a grin, smiling but somehow menacing. Then the dream begins. I'm now seated in a large, nicely decorated living room with a dramatic carved stone fireplace and sparkling chandelier above my head. There are even fresh-cut flowers in a glass vase on the large oak table across the room. I've never seen anything quite so magnificent. I look down and realize I'm dressed in finery: a bright blue velvet jacket with gold buttons, crisp white hose, and shiny black shoes with brass buckles. In my right hand is a fine crystal goblet.

As I lift it to my lips and take a sip, I savor the warming sweetness of port. Resting on the side table to my left is a smooth walnut church warden pipe and red leather tobacco pouch with initials embroidered "JP." Is this me?

As it is with dreams, I'm now outside the house surveying the building and the surrounding landscape. I cannot believe my eyes. It's Meg's house. A brick-built manor house with black wooden frame, three tall chimneys, leaded glass windows, and a carved solid oak front door with a large brass knocker at its center. A truly magnificent sight!

I turn around to survey my surroundings: rows of hops in full bloom as far as my eyes can see.

As I fully absorb my situation, I'm awakened by my neighbor's cockerel.

Could this be possible? Could this be my future?

The following evening, I turn the handle of the heavy oak door of the Fox Inn. I am overwhelmed by conflicting feelings of exhilaration and trepidation. Coming in from the late summer's evening sunlight, my eyes adjust to the darkness inside. Nervously, I scan the public bar in search of my mysterious benefactor, but he is nowhere to be seen. After ordering my usual mug of ale, I take my favorite seat in the window and await in anticipation. My taste buds recall the sweetness of the port from my dream as the bitterness of the ale no longer satisfies. The bar is still empty but for myself and Will behind the bar. We are both silent. Minutes feel like hours as my mind races. What is happening? Is this real?

"Good evening to you, Mr. Price!"

I turn to see him sitting by the fire just as the previous evening. Has he been there all along? It seems that he magically appeared from nowhere.

"Well hello."

How does he know my surname? I never told him. Am I crazy?

"So, you have slept on my proposition and decided on moving forward; am I correct, Jack?"

"Yes, I have." Despite the ale, my mouth is like cotton wool. I can only respond in a few words.

"Then let us proceed with the contract."

"Contract?'"

"Indeed, this is a binding contract. Which we both must sign."

An ancient looking piece of parchment is placed in front of me as he hands me a quill pen and unscrews a small silver container. I dip the pen into the ink, which appears to be bright scarlet, and I read my contract…

"In return for sufficient gold to provide me a life of luxury, I, Jack Price Esq., will on my sixtieth birthday give up my soul to Bernael Le Ciffre."

"Why on my sixtieth birthday?"

"Don't you want a long life to enjoy your wealth?" Another answer with a question!

"Of course."

I sign my name, and he signs his. Simple. Done.

He appears to fade away, but then I realize that the whole scene is changing and before I know it I'm seated alone again, but now it feels totally different.

"Happy birthday, Mr. Price."

It's Will calling from behind the bar.

"Oh! Thanks, Will."

"How old am I?" I think. I reach into my pocket to look for a clue, and after pulling out keys and a handkerchief, I find a diary. Flipping through the pages filled with business meetings and events, I see the date and quickly calculate that I am forty years old.

"Thank heavens I'm not sixty yet."

"Hah! You'll be lucky if you make fifty with your drinking, Jack. That brandy'll do you in, mark my words."

I realize my thoughts are being spoken aloud!

Reflecting on my current situation, I realize that it all really happened. I have now been the owner of Meg's farm for ten years and have every luxury that I could have dreamed. In fact, I am reminded of my dream the night of my fortuitous meeting with my mysterious stranger, Mr. Le Ciffre. I am now living that dream!

"How's the 'arvest this year, Jack? Another good un, I'll wager!"

"Couldn't be better, Will. Made over twenty guineas again just like the past three years and now I have enough in the bank to buy another farm. I put an offer in on Bramley Manor, and I'm thinking Lord Warburton is going to take it. Imagine me as Lord of the Manor. Jack Price who came from nowhere and had nowt to his name!"

Life could not have been better for me.

"Happy birthday, Jack!"

I look up to see my good friend and business partner, John Wall. Looking fine and dandy as always.

"Good day to you, sir! It's a fine day is it not?"

"Well, I have to report that the factory is running according to plan and the orders are flooding in, so in that respect indeed it is a fine day!"

"Good to hear, my dearest friend. I cannot believe that it was ten years almost to the day that we sat here with William Davis and devised an experiment that has become such a success. The Worcester Tonquin Manufactory is indeed a model of manufacturing perfection."

"Aye and so it is, Jack. I hark back many a time to our walks on the Malvern Hills, you and I, back and forth, sharing ideas, deliberating and debating and imagining something quite unique, something magical. I never imagined in my wildest dreams that those walks and talks could transpose to such an incredible venture."

"'Tis surely true, John. Though it's been way too long since you and I walked the hills; we must get back out there. There's a mystery in them hills that I'm convinced is the essence to imagination."

"Too deep for me, Jack! Me thinks you're in need of a birthday beverage. What's your poison?"

"Poison forsooth! Seeing as you're offering and it's my birthday and all, I'll take a brandy, the devil-take me!"

"That he will, Jack! Mark my words. You're a mischievous spirit, but you've a heart of gold. I'm often telling folks of your innovations at the hopyard. Nobody that I know is so thoughtful and caring of their workers. And look at the results; my, you've the best run business in the county, I'll swear."

"You're a kind friend. I must say, I may have come from nothing, but I've long recognized that the key to success is taking good care of your workers. Let's face it, without them we're nothing."

"'Tis true, but you have also set a new standard in English gardens with your walled garden. I have not seen the like anywhere. A radical approach to gardens, totally unlike the French formality. You have foxgloves, lupine, hollyhocks, and thistles all mixed in, just like nature made them. Gorgeous! But I dally—there's a brandy waiting for you!"

As warm and homely as I feel, the room again starts to fade away, and I'm already shifting to another time.

I now find myself lying in bed with blankets pulled up to my neck. I'm in a large ornate four poster bed with deep maroon velvet curtains enclosing it. Lifting up my right hand

I see it is old and wrinkled with blue veins protruding. I am old. My breathing is shallow and slow. I hear the bedroom door handle turn, the creak as it opens, then footsteps crossing the floor.

"Who is it?" I whimper.

"'Tis only I, Jack: Bernael."

"Oh my god!" I scream as I see two hands reaching in and pulling the bed curtains apart—thin pale hands with long, pointed fingernails. Through clouded eyes, I recognize his face.

"What you doin' 'ere?"

"I have come for my payment."

I feel myself lifting up from my bed as though I'm floating. Then the curtains disappear, and I see my bedroom full of grey figures, with ghostly faces, writhing in agony.

"James? It's time to come back. You're safe now." I heard the voice of Mr. Kardac close by as my eyes opened fully. It took me a few moments to calm myself and gather my thoughts.

"Owen Rees, Orlando Pryce, and now Jack Price?" Kardac questioned.

"How do you know of Jack Price?"

"You're not aware, but during your regression, you talk. You share each and every experience as it happens. I've taken copious notes and have it all down here."

"But it really happened, or am I just imagining it all?"

"Could it be possible that your subconscious could create such a story? Perhaps, but unlikely. Past life experiences are more real than most accept. It can be quite challenging, if not shocking, to know that you may have lived a prior life."

"But I did play in the hopyards when I was young. Maybe that's just my memory creating a story?"

"Of course, that is possible. Though in your case, I would say the details are not those of mere imagination."

"But what then of the fact that all three of my experiences resulted in giving up my soul? What does that mean?"

"Life is a constant battle between good and evil, nothing more. Your experiences are proof of that fact."

"But three! Am I damned?"

"No, not damned. But opening up to a reality that once was beyond your comprehension. Though you may have chosen the dark side in those past lives, that does not mean you continued to do so or that your soul is eternally damned. We should continue to explore and uncover your subsequent lives. Only then will we know."

"Though I am amazed to be saying so, that actually makes a lot of sense. I'd never have imagined myself sitting here saying that."

"It is destiny that brought you to me."

With that, I left and headed home for a much-needed good night's sleep.

Chapter Eight

My sessions with Mr. Kardac rarely left my mind. It was as if I were living multiple lives in different times and just couldn't let go or focus on my day-to-day life. What troubled me more than anything was not knowing if this was all in my imagination—merely stories that I'd subconsciously fabricated based upon conscious memories—or if there were some reality to them. I was determined to break through this dilemma and resolved to conduct my own research. Part of me felt like a fool, imagining that these could have been actual real people, but my experiences in Mr. Kardac's office were so vivid. And what about my visit to Orlando Pryce's tomb? Certainly, there was some proof there, but had I read his name when I was young and forgotten about it? I needed to find out more about Orlando Pryce and confirm the existence of Owen Rees and Jack Price, else I'd continue to spin. So, I decided to take the following Monday off work, it was a quiet day anyway, and plan a day in Worcester digging into the archives at the county office of births and deaths. It appeared that all three—Owen Rees, Orlando Pryce, and Jack Price—spent parts of their lives in and around Worcester, so that seemed to be the right place to start.

When Monday came around, I still felt like a fool but persisted in my venture and headed down to the city in which I was born.

By 9:15 a.m. I was in the Worcestershire office of births and deaths. After filling out a couple of procedural forms and showing my driving license as personal identification, I was ushered into the archives. Down in the depths of the Victorian building, the main records section was a dimly lit, vast cave-like room. Filing cabinets were arranged in lines and each section sorted by surname.

As I searched for the section beginning with "R," I found that my hands were beginning to sweat and my heart was pounding.

"This is silly!" I said to myself.

Nothing will come if it.

Filtering through drawers of filing cards, I narrowed down to "Rees" and then realized there were hundreds! However, it was only a few minutes before I came upon an "Owen Rees" and pulled out the filing card.

"Born of Dylan and Gwyneth Rees in the parish of St. John's Worcester the year of our Lord 1356, Owen James Rees. Died of natural causes in Bransford, Worcestershire in the year 1416."

Dropping the card, I felt faint and reached for the cabinet beside me to steady myself.

"You alright, sir?" A voice came from behind me.

"Oh, I'm fine. Thanks for asking though."

But I was anything but fine; I was in complete shock. I had now confirmed the existence of Owen Rees. Now, I wanted more information about Orlando Pryce and to confirm that Jack Price lived. I returned Owen Rees's card and quickly walked to the "P" section to continue my investigation.

"Orlando, born in the parish of Powick, just outside Worcester in 1586 and died in the city of Worcester in 1666."

I then found Jack's card under his Christian name on record, John. Born in Bromyard in 1721; died in his home in Bransford in 1781.

They all three were real!

I needed a drink.

After thanking the registrar and signing out, I couldn't wait to light up a cigarette as I walked to my car. I sat on the bench at the side of the car park and finished my smoke before leaving the car park.

Driving down Deansway, I passed All Saints Church and turned left towards Broad Street and crossed the bridge over the River Severn. I took a quick glance to my left to see the cathedral majestically overlooking the river. Without really thinking, I recognized I was on my way along the Bransford Road passing by woods and hopyards. Crossing the River Teme bridge, the Fox Inn came into view, sitting as it had for hundreds of years, just off the main road to the left-hand side.

Having parked just behind the pub, I entered through the back door and walked towards the bar.

"Good day, sir!" the landlord greeted me.

"Oh, yes, good day to you too," I stuttered.

"You okay, sir? Look like you've seen a ghost."

"Might be truer than you realize," I mumbled to myself. "No, I'm fine," I responded, "just in need of a pint of bitter, please."

"Ah well, that I can do for you. Davenports?"

"Absolutely!"

As he poured my beer, I sat at the bar and pondered. What next? I thought. But I'd been almost unconsciously drawn to Bransford, so perhaps I should dig around a little more?

"Is Meg's Farm near here?" I inquired, trying to sound nonchalant.

"Meg's Farm? No, never heard of it, sir."

"It's a pretty decent-sized hopyard, about fifty-nine acres, I'd say, with an early seventeenth century house; actually, more like a manor house."

"Hmm! Let me think." He paused and continued drying glasses; then after a minute or so, he continued. "Now that I think of it, that sounds more like Price Manor. Yes, I'd say it is, almost certainly. Just a mile down the country lane behind the pub, alongside the river. Mind if I ask why you're looking for it, sir? Don't mean to intrude, but there's been no one living there for these past ten years. Run-down, it is. Sorry state."

Struggling for a believable explanation, I replied, "I heard it was up for sale and thought I'd take a quick look before talking to the estate agent."

"Ah! Good idea. Those estate agents will convince you to buy anything! Best to look at it first. Like I say, nice piece of land, but needs a fair amount of work. Another pint, sir?"

"No, thank you though. I'd best be on my way."

The drive along the riverside was beautiful, pastoral England at its best. Within a few minutes. I passed a tattered old sign on the right: "Price Manor."

Reversing a few yards, I backed into the driveway in front of the wrought iron gate and parked the car. The gate was chained and padlocked, but I could get a good view of the manor house through the bars of the gate. It looked quite magnificent. I looked up at the bedroom window and pictured Jack there inside encountering Bernael for the final time.

"No, no, no!" I said aloud. "It's impossible!"

After a morning of revelations, I felt somewhat overwhelmed; my head was spinning and I needed to clear my mind. As a teenager, my haven for peace and clarity was always British Camp, one of the Malvern Hills. Although an ancient British fort, dating back to the Iron Age, all that remained was a series of concentric earth mounds, but to me it had a mystical energy and a deep connection. The perfect place to reflect and reconnect.

The drive meandering through the quaint Worcestershire villages, steeped in history, then along the narrow country roads, was both beautiful and relaxing.

As I entered Great Malvern, I passed by the Winter Gardens, and recalled one of the great concerts I'd been to there in the early seventies. In 1972, Mott the Hoople had suddenly become huge with the success of the David Bowie composition "All the Young Dudes." I had previously followed them as a local Hereford band for many years, but they'd never made it until Bowie gave them a hit. They did turn a bit "glam," but you had to do what you had to do in the seventies!

After parking just below British Camp, I briskly hiked up the pathway, stopping twice to catch my breath before I reached the top. At the summit, I turned around and around, surveying and soaking in the countryside of Herefordshire to the one side and Worcestershire to the other. In the far distance I could pick out the cathedral and to the other side the Brecon Beacons of Wales. It was just as I remembered it; absolutely gorgeous.

Well prepared, I had my portable cassette player and earphones with me, and once I'd found a nice, soft spot of grass, I sat down to relax. Putting on the earphones, I pressed play and lay back to the opening chords of "The Lark Ascending" by Ralph Vaughan Williams. The violin perfectly captured the soaring and chirping of the skylark, a common sight over the Malvern Hills, hovering high up above and singing merrily.

Absorbed in the music, my mind began to clear as the recent events started to fall into place. The connections were incredible. Owen, Orlando, and Jack each had frequented my favorite pub in Worcester: The Cardinal's Hat. Owen and Orlando were both tightly connected to the cathedral, just as I had been. Then Jack spent his life in the hopyards of Bransford and walked the Malvern Hills with his partner, John Wall—both of which were my favorite places to escape from the stresses of the world. As complicated and shocking as it all seemed, there was a pattern forming.

I must have drifted off to sleep, as the next thing I knew, *Five Variants of Dives and Lazarus*, another Vaughan Williams masterpiece of rural England, was drawing to a close.

The sun was settling down towards the Brecon Beacons, casting a light mauve hue over the fields below.

"Time for a pint!" I decided.

At the foot of the hill, the Malvern Hills Hotel had been a gathering place for walkers since Victorian times, and it was to be my early evening repose.

They had Marston's Pedigree on cask, so I was happy. Taking a seat at the bar, I ordered my beer and a sandwich, as I realized I'd not eaten since early breakfast. It had been that kind of day—a day of revelations and connections, when food becomes an afterthought. After three pints and a second roast beef sandwich, I made my way home listening to Pink Floyd's "Echoes" and went straight to an early bed.

Chapter Nine

NED PRIESTLY

(1783–1805)

ON MONDAY MORNING, I CALLED KARDAC AND SCHEDULED my next appointment. He easily convinced me to plan on three more sessions, as he believed that would complete our analysis, plus he heavily discounted his fees for three sessions, charging only for two. Hard to resist!

I had started to look forward to my Thursday evenings with Kardac, and the weekdays tended to drag, feeling almost unimportant in comparison to my time in analysis. It was almost as though I was becoming more connected and intrigued with these past lives than my current, somewhat mundane life.

Later that week, seated in what was becoming my favorite chair, I was soon shifted into a different time.

I feel unsteady and nauseous. I am swaying and holding tight to a wooden post. My sight clears and I look down to what looks like a hundred feet below me. The deck of a sailing ship. I now hear cannon fire, and smoke drifts across the water below me. Clearing my eyes, I see another sailing ship close to our leeward side, its cannons firing back at us. The shock wave hits, and I feel the shudder of a broadside.

I come to my senses and look across at the opposing ship to see three marines poised to fire from their crow's nest. Looking down to our mizzen deck, through the smoke, I can pick out their targets: our Admiral and his officers standing in a group, delivering orders to our crew.

I raise my musket to my right shoulder and take careful aim at one of the French marines. Aiming for his chest, I am about to fire when I see three puffs of smoke; all three have fired. Looking down, I see our Admiral fall to the deck.

I fire and watch as my target drops his musket, clutches his chest, and falls from his perch.

My position is now compromised, and the remaining two adversaries are busily reloading. One prepares to aim at me while the other looks down towards our Captain who is leaning over our stricken Admiral.

I have a choice: save my Captain or save myself.

The scene fades away and shifts. I'm now standing at a bar in a small smoky pub with black beams crossing the low ceiling. The white paint is stained yellow from the smoke, and the small coal fire is ablaze, adding more smoke to the room. Looking around me, I see groups of old men in working clothes and a young woman sitting at a small round table. She's looking towards me: she has dark hair falling loosely to her shoulders, bright green eyes, and a lovely smile, which appears to be directed at me.

"I'll have a cider, luv." She is speaking to me.

"Right o, luv. Pint or 'arf?"

"Do you know me, Ned Priestly? When did I ever settle for an 'arf?"

"Silly me! Of course, Evelynn."

"Well, at least you remember my name. You looked like you was in another world for a minute then. Welcome back, Ned!"

Carrying my beer and her cider over to our table, I sit down beside her as she leans over and kisses my cheek.

"There, luv! I think you needed that. Cheers!"

"I'm always in need of a kiss from you, Evelynn Morton. That I am!"

"Plenty more where that came from if you plays your cards right. She nudges me and winks."

"Feels like the old days don't it, luv. Remember when we'd sneak out of school at mid-day break and come over here for a drink?"

"Yeah! And we'd spend our lunch money on a bun from the baker's and a beer, instead of eating in the school canteen? We was mischievous little kids, wasn't we?"

"If memory recalls, you was only thirteen then, and I was a grown up fourteen! We did have some good times, didn't we?"

"Always Ned, always did and always do, even though we're supposed to be grown-ups now."

"I loved our weekend walks on the Malverns. I felt like that was our place. Walking hand in hand without a care in the world."

"Still don't have a care in the world, or are you still fretting over joining up and going to sea?"

"Feels like my duty, luv. The country's at war and needs people like me. How can I sit here and not do my part?"

"I'm your part, Ned Priestly, and don't you forget it! Though I do understand. Harry joined up last week and Will Smith too. Soon Ledbury'll be dead as a doornail. All you lads gone to fight."

I put my arm round her should and draw her towards me for another kiss.

Then the room fades away again.

I hear a whistle blowing and then a drum roll. I'm standing shoulder to shoulder with a group of men. Glancing to my right and left, I see we are all dressed in naval clothing, all facing towards a raised deck above an arched wooden door. Stooping as he comes from the door is a tall man dressed in a finely embroidered uniform of deep blue. He raises a hat to his head as he turns up the steps to the upper deck. This must be the captain?

"Lieutenant Quilliam, proceed with the orders of the day, if you will." His accent is refined and his tone sensitive and almost tentative.

"Aye, aye, Captain Hardy," the man standing by his side booms out, he certainly not being tentative.

"Quartermaster, daily rations if you will?"

"Yes sir!" The voice belongs to a young lad hardly older than me. "Daily ration: six pints of ale, half a pint of rum with lemon to prevent the scurvy, sir. Breakfast of burgoo porridge and molasses and dinner of salted beef and pork fried peas. Aft gun crew be cooking for the day."

"Thank you, Quartermaster. Let us now proceed with the discipline of the day, Lieutenant Quilliam," the captain almost whispers.

"Aye, aye, Captain," he bellows.

"Able seaman Harding. Step forward."

A young lad looking no more than fifteen steps out of the line and slowly walks towards the mast in front of us. Two marines put down their muskets and wrestle him forward, binding his hands behind the mast.

"For the crime of theft, this man is sentenced to twenty lashes. Proceed with the punishment."

I watch as his back is flayed by the cat-o'-nine-tails and his blood splashes onto the deck. He sobs but doesn't cry out or resist, showing he's a man in front of his shipmates. His crime was stealing a loaf of bread from the quartermaster's store. Does that warrant twenty lashes? Perhaps not in normal society, but we are on a man-of-war where discipline is essential.

As they untie his hands, he initially slumps to the deck; then with pride he stands straight and returns to the ranks. I'm impressed by his resolve.

"Able seamen Wilkins, step forward for your punishment."

Looking to my left, I see an older man with a craggy face and scruffy look about him slowly step out towards the mast.

"For the crime of dereliction of duty and insubordination, able seaman Wilkins, you are sentenced to run the gauntlet. Having refused to do your duty to haul in the top sails during yesterday's heavy winds, your shipmates were required to take over your duties, and thus they will administer the punishment."

The marines step forward and hand each of us a knitted rope.

"Line up!" Lieutenant Quilliam barks out, with a level of glee in his voice.

We all shuffle to form two lines facing one another while holding the ropes in our hands.

"Walk forth, Wilkins."

He slowly shuffles between the lines as the ropes flail over his back and his sides. He covers his head with his hands and squeals, moving faster to make it to the end of the line. He is not a popular shipmate, thus the blows fly heavily on him.

As he passes me, he smirks, and my normal calm quickly changes to anger as I thrash my rope hard across his head.

All goes quiet and then the lieutenant speaks.

"Captain Hardy, sir. Orders of the day, sir."

"Thank you, Mister Quilliam."

"Lads, I cannot say otherwise, but today we will assuredly experience a battle unlike any other before. The French and Spanish fleet may outnumber us and outgun us, but they do not have you, my band of brothers. Your gunnery is superb, your accuracy and rate of fire unmatched. Your discipline under fire is impeccable. More than that, you are English to the core and as such will never, ever, give in, to the last man. With the grace of God and a fair wind we will prevail."

Suddenly there is total silence.

His Lordship, Admiral Nelson, calmly walks from his cabin. Jacket sleeve pinned across his chest and black patch covering one eye, he is unmistakable. He greets Second Lieutenant Pasco on the poop deck with a flick of his forefinger to his forehead.

"Mr. Pasco, I wish to say to the fleet, 'ENGLAND CONFIDES THAT EVERY MAN WILL DO HIS DUTY.' You must be quick, for I have one more to make, which is for close action."

Mr. Pasco replies, "If your Lordship will permit me to substitute 'expects' for 'confides,' the signal will soon be completed because the word 'expects' is in the vocabulary, and 'confides' must be spelt."

His Lordship replies, in haste, and with seeming satisfaction, "That will do, Pasco, make it so directly."

As the signal flags are running up the mizzenmast, Captain Hardy and Lieutenant Quilliam confer; then Quilliam steps forward to address the full crew. All eight hundred of us are cramped onto the main decks, awaiting the battle orders before running to our posts. With 104 guns on three-gun decks, we are formidable. My job, as a marine sharpshooter atop the crow's nest, is to protect our officers on the deck a hundred feet below, while harassing the enemy officers.

Lieutenant Quilliam begins the orders of the day. "Vice-Admiral Collingwood will be leading our lee column aboard the *Royal Sovereign*. We on HMS *Victory* will lead our windward column. Our strategy is to cut the enemy line into three and with superior firepower overwhelm them.

"Our Admiral has requested we send clear messages to all captains and crew that 'No captain can do very wrong if he places his ship alongside that of the enemy.' In short, as this battle commences, circumstances will shift, and each ship must make their own decisions on their execution of engagement.

"To attain maximum speed, we will maintain full sails, including stuns'ls until we engage the enemy.

"Battle stations, crew!" he screams and turns back towards Nelson and Hardy.

As the wind is light, the going is slow, even with all sails. I lift my musket and tighten the leather strap across my chest as I embark on my climb up the rigging towards the crow's nest. Fearing heights, this is my least favorite time; though strangely enough, once at the top, I feel quite calm and almost safe. Perhaps this is due to the peace and quite high above the decks. All I hear is the whistle of the wind through the rigging and the high-pitched squawks of seagulls hovering around me.

From my position, I have a perfect view of the leeward column. The *Royal Sovereign* is outrunning the rest of the line, likely due to its recent bottom cleaning.

They're now coming under heavy, raking fire from the enemy line, but their fast pace takes them through the line, while the slower second ship takes the brunt of the enemy fire. The *Belleisle* is engaged by the *Aigle*, the *Achille*, and the *Fougueux*. Within minutes, she is completely dismasted, unable to maneuver, and largely unable to fight, as her sails blind her batteries. But she keeps her flag flying while her fellow ships come to her aid.

We are now under fire from the *Redoutable*, the *Santisima Trinidad*, the *Héros*, and the *Neptune*. Thankfully, their accuracy is poor and their rate of fire low, but still I look down to see numbers of our crew hit by grapeshot. Time seems to slow as we slowly creep towards the enemy line, and finally after what feels an eternity, we glide between the *Redoutable* and the *Bucentaure*.

We fire a full broadside into the stern of the *Bucentaure*, and through the smoke it appears her stern is completely shattered.

Now we are steering into the wind, slowing and coming aside the *Redoutable*. Our following ships are now taking on the *Bucentaure*.

I hold tight on the rigging, anticipating our next broadside. All forty-eight port guns let loose in perfect unison, creating a thunderous shudder through the ship, and I feel the main mast leaning away to starboard.

We are now locked up alongside the *Redoutable* as I see crowds of marines in their main deck making ready to board us. I can finally get to work. The officers are obscured by the wreckage from their mast and main sail, but I can pick off the marine officers with ease.

Our *Temeraire* now pulls around astern of the *Redoutable* and, firing a broadside, takes their decks. The French marines almost disintegrate in front of my eyes as bodies fly everywhere. Their boarding is thwarted, but then through the cacophony I hear a crack, which I immediately recognize as a French sharpshooter. Looking down to our deck, I see our Admiral clutch his shoulder and fall back. Nelson is hit!

Raising my musket, I pick out the puff of smoke from the assassin and take aim. Three slow breaths to calm myself, and I squeeze my trigger. As the recoil hits my shoulder, I am rewarded with the view of the French sharpshooter falling. Reloading quickly, I can see his partner taking aim towards Captain Hardy, who is protectively leaning over our injured Admiral. In the nick of time, my shot is perfect, and I have saved my Captain.

Then I am hit by a sudden thump to my chest. I drop my musket and clutch the rigging as through the smoke I see my assailant already reloading.

With my free hand, I reach into my inside pocket and pull out a small, crumpled photograph; the last thing I see on this earth is my love, my Evelynn.

"Seems to me that you just experienced the Battle of Trafalgar! Nelson's famous and final victory over the French and Spanish combined fleets. Unfortunately, you were also present at his demise; shot through the spine by a French sniper's bullet." It was Kardac's voice, bringing me back to reality.

"It was so vivid, it was as if I were there."

"Perhaps you were."

"At least there was no devil in disguise this time," I replied, only half-jokingly.

"This gives me a very strong feeling that we are transitioning into a new phase of your past lives. Clearly you forfeited your life in the selfless interest of another. That is highly significant."

"That makes sense, though I have to process it before I'm convinced. But it does suggest one thing: my nightmares about and fear of heights. In my dreams, I often fall from a high and hazardous place, usually without anything to cling to."

"Exactly! You are making the connections quite perfectly, my friend. Let's call it a day for now, or I should more accurately say let's call it a night, as it is past 9:00 p.m. and time for my bed, if not for yours."

He was correct in that it was late for him, but I needed a drink before my night was concluded.

Once home, I thoroughly enjoyed an Ardbeg before bed, reflecting on the Battle of Trafalgar, but also wondering about the girl in my story. Who was she?

Chapter Ten

MILTON PROSSER

(1805–1849)

THE FOLLOWING THURSDAY, I WAS MEANDERING THROUGH early evening rush hour traffic on my way into the city center for my next session. Wondering what might come up that evening, I'd started to become more and more interested in exploring what could be my past. Was I becoming addicted or attached to things that never happened and were simply a part of my deep subconscious? Or could they possibly have been my past lives and real?

Richard Preece

On the way into town I listened to "John Barleycorn" by Traffic, which somehow settled my spirit and connected me to my past.

What would be in store for me tonight? I wondered. Would it be a return to visits from the devil? I was starting to wonder if this truly was a battle between good and evil.

It was quiet on Bank Street that evening, so I was able to park right outside Kardac's building. I smoked a Dunhill on the doorstep, being a few minutes premature. Flicking the butt into the gutter, I turned and bumped into a young woman leaving the building.

"Oh! I'm sorry!" I apologized. I couldn't help but notice how attractive she looked.

"Never mind, dear," she said, smiling as she passed me by.

I stopped and waited as she walked to her car. It was an Austin Healey, my second favorite car. She opened her car door, then looked back straight at me and smiled again before getting in and starting up the engine.

"Odd," I thought. I felt like I knew her.

On my now favorite chair, I listened to Kardac counting down as I breathed deeply and relaxed.

I am in the dark, with just a glimmer of light from what appears to be a small oil lamp. As my eyes adjust, the lamp casts flickering shadows on the walls around me. No, not walls but shiny black coal; I'm in a coal mine.

Looking around me to get my bearings, I am alone. As my eyes sweep around in a circle, it becomes evident that there is no entrance or exit. I am trapped. With the lamp in my right hand, I survey the coal face, closely feeling for gaps, only to find what once was the exit is filled top to bottom with large blocks of coal and rock. As I begin to remove rocks and coal and cast them behind me, I am confronted by more and more. I lift the cover from my lamp and move it slowly across the fallen rubble, hoping for a draft to indicate a gap. The flame does not even flicker; there is no draft. I realize there is no escape.

Sitting down on a heap of rocks in the total silence, I can only hear the drips of water seeping through the coal face. It is frigidly cold and damp. I am alone and trapped. My lamp light fades, and I am left in blackness.

The scene transforms, and I'm now walking down a street lined on both sides by brick houses. Each has a small front door with one dirty window next to it; looking up, I see just two small windows above, each covered in dirty grey grime.

I hear my boots clicking on the stone pavement as a horse and cart rattles by loaded with milk churns.

Many other men, dressed in filthy worn jackets and trousers covered in black dust, are now walking along both sides of the street. They're carrying small sacks over their shoulders, each with a metal lamp hanging and clanging from their leather belts.

"'Ow am yer, Milt? Is you cummin' to the Duke?"

I turn and look over my shoulder to see a short skinny lad with straggly red hair all coated in black.

"Alright, Jimmy. 'Ows you doin', our kid?"

I hear my voice and it sounds strange. The accent is thick and yammy. I must be somewhere in the Black Country of the West Midlands.

"First un is on me, Milt!"

"That'll be a first. Hah!" I laughed then started coughing and hacking up phlegm.

"That coal dust'll get yer. You needs a good pint o' mild, my little luv."

Richard Preece

Slapping him on the shoulder, I spit into the gutter as we both turn into the open doorway of the Duke of Wellington.

The bar is full of miners looking just like us, covered in dust and grime. We squeeze our way to the bar and order our beers, dropping our sacks on the floor.

"Cheers, Mabel!"

"Cheers, Milt!"

"'Ow's yer cockin'em?"

"Ones and twos, Mabel! Hah!" I start hacking again and lean down to spit into the metal bowl below the bar.

"Yer a right one, Milton Prosser. 'Arkin back to when you was a toddler, yer mum'd say you 'ad the face of an angel with a mind full a mischief! Never a truer word spoke. But yer a luvly lad, give us a kiss!"

Leaning over the bar, I give Mabel a big smacker on her lips and a naughty wink.

"Luvly!" she says with a sigh.

"'O'right, Milt! 'Ows yer old man doin'? 'Ent sin 'im in donkey's."

"Still down them pits on the old face. Sick of it though 'e is. Grumpy old fart, when 'e ent grumblin' 'bout work 'e's goin' on about the 'ouse."

"That be 'Arry! Not one to look on the bright side. An' he's right about 'ouses; walls like cardboard, full of damp, privies always blocking up, and they never cleans them windows. Can't see out a' mine 'cos of the soot."

"Right, Will. Lilleshall don't take much care of our 'ouses. 'Spect they'd rather save the cash. Just like the mines: they ain't fixed the lift on pit three and none of the fans ever work. Always smells of gas down there."

"Aye! We'd all in for a catastrophe, that's what I'd say."

"Fancy words, Will. 'Catastrophe,' eh? Where'd you learn that one—not at school 'cos you never went!"

"Books, my young Milt. Books from the church library. At least Vicar Jones takes a care of 'is flock. You bin singin' of late?"

"Aye. Every Sunday. Vicar says I could sing for the Worcester festival. I might just try that one day."

"Fancy that! Colliery lad from Donnington Wood singing with the hoity-toities!"

"Ain't 'appen'd yet! But I'm thinkin' of goin' to auditions in Worcester next month. We'll see."

With that, I pull out a clay pipe and pouch of tobacco from my jacket pocket, fill my pipe, and start puffing away.

"'Nother pint, Milt?" It's Jimmy tugging at my sleeve.

"It's Friday en' it? Course. Night's young yet."

"'Ow's yer mum, by the way?" Jimmy asks as he hands me another pint of mild.

"Still doin' 'er sewin' and makin' ends meet, though I think she's gettin' sick of it. Not much dosh in sewin' clothes these days. Who can afford 'em? Though she did do a fancy wedding dress last month and made a bit. Lovely it were. 'Twas for Jessica Hawkins."

"Jessie Hawkins got wed? I'll be! I used to go out of 'er. Right goer she were."

"Better keep that to yourself, Jimmy. I hear her husband's a boxer!" I say, laughing.

"Talkin' of weddin's, when's you and Lizzie gonna tie the knot, Milt?"

"Puttin' money aside for the ring. Gonna pop the question this autumn."

"She's a keeper, that's fer sure! Luvly lass that Lizzie Martin."

"Aye, face of an angel and a 'eart of gold. Ain't a finer woman in this world for me."

"You workin' Lodge Pit still, Milt?"

I turn round to see Davy Smith with a big broad smile on his face.

"Aye, these past six months. Stinking hole it is. Dripping with water and reeks of gas."

"I 'ears them Lancashire lads are goin' on strike 'cos of the workin' conditions."

"Good luck to 'em, I say. Like as not they'll all lose their jobs and be put out in the street."

"Too true, whilst the bosses make a mint."

"Back in a jiffy, I'm gone for a pee."

As I walk towards the toilets out behind the pub, my vision turns bleary and then fades away.

I first sense a musty smell, then hear singing, as my vision comes back. Standing in front of a huge, carved oak door, I'm looking at a list of names posted on the wall.

Scanning the list, I see my name mid-way down: "Milton Prosser 12:10 p.m."

I am at the Three Choirs Festival audition. Putting my eye to the door, I can hear a beautiful voice: the deep rich tones of a good tenor.

"I'm not close to that," I whisper.

"You'll not know 'til you try, now will you lad?"

I realize I spoke out loud. Blushing with embarrassment at being caught with my ear to the door, I turn around to see a benevolent smile. A quick look confirms that I'm standing in front of a church minister dressed in a long black robe with a large gold cross hanging from his neck.

"Oh! I'm sorry. I didn't realize you was there. I apologize."

"No matter, young man. To whom am I speaking?" he asks very formally.

"Milton Prosser, sir."

"No 'sir' please, just Colin will suffice," he replies.

Leaning towards the list of names, he points to my name. "Looks like you're up next then. Here just in time, I'd say."

With that said, he opens the door and walks in confidently.

"Good afternoon, Thomas. I am delivering Milton Prosser for his audition. I believe you'll find him a fine addition to the chorus."

Sitting at the piano, a man looks up and gestures to me to come forward.

"Thank you, Colin. Do you know this young man?"

"No. We just met, but I'm a good judge of character as you know."

"Well then, Milton, what are you singing today?"

"Beg yer pardon, sir, but I'd like to start with the 'Old Hundredth' if that be acceptable."

"Most acceptable, I'd say. One of my favorite hymns."

I am standing next to the piano as he begins the introduction. I swallow hard a couple of times to clear my throat and begin to sing. Nervously at first, my voice sounds thin and croaky, but as I move into the third line, my confidence grows and I feel my voice strengthen.

"Him serve with mirth, His praise forth tell / Come ye before Him and rejoice."

With each line my voice resonates and echoes around the walls.

For my second piece I sing "Cwm Rhondda."

> *"Guide me, O thou great Redeemer,*
> *Pilgrim through this barren land;*
> *I am weak, but thou art mighty;*
> *Hold me with thy powerful hand:*
> *Bread of heaven, bread of heaven*
> *Feed me till I want no more.*
> *Feed me till I want no more."*

Now fully engrossed in my singing, I hardly notice the minister standing across the floor nodding and smiling.

As the final line fades away, the minister claps his hands.

"Wonderful, Milton. Don't you think, Thomas?"

"Candidly, Colin, I am quite amazed. With honest humility, I must confess I never expected such a voice from a lad from the coal mines."

"Milton, I hope you will do us the honor of joining our chorus."

"Couldn't think of anything finer," I say with a huge grin.

"Then please take the practice schedule; there's one on the table there. We begin in two weeks' time with Mendelssohn's *Elijah*; I think you'll find it to your liking, Milton."

"Good day to you, sir."

"God bless you, sir." I tip my finger to my forehead, turn on my heels, and leave with the schedule in my hand. My heart is pounding with excitement and joy.

Again, my sight becomes blurry, then fades away quickly.

The joy disintegrates immediately as I am now back in the coal mine, feeling cold and miserable, sensing a noxious odor of gas.

I am on my knees hacking away at the coal face with a small pickax. As sweat dribbles into my eyes, I wipe them with my hand, only to smear coal dust into my eyes.

"Nearly time for nosh," I hear, and through the dim light of my lamp I see Jimmy close by.

"Good job! I could eat a horse."

"Knowing yer, mum, that might not be far from the truth!" Jimmy says, laughing.

"What's on earth's that?" I scream, as a loud, deep rumbling sound rolls towards us.

"Holy shite!" Jimmy exclaims, jumping to his feet.

Dust starts pouring towards us as the beams above the entrance tunnel creak and crack like matchsticks. The roof starts to cave in and then there is an eerie stillness.

"Cum on, Jimmy, let's get out."

But then I see Jimmy lies flat. As I look over him and hold my lamp closer, I see blood pouring down his cheek. He must have been hit on the head. He is out cold. I shake his shoulder and he mumbles.

The beams start to creak again. I grab Jimmy around his shoulders and start to drag him down the tunnel. Even though he's no big lad, it's tough going as I drag him along. I hear voices, and then helping hands grab him and pull him away.

"We've got 'im, Milt. Let's get out of 'ere afore it caves in."

"I gotta get me sack. Ain't leaving Lizzie's wedding ring—askin' 'er 'and next week," I say, turning and heading back down the tunnel.

Just as I reach for my sack, the beams crack again and the whole tunnel disappears.

I'm back where I started. I should feel panic, but whether it's having saved my best friend, Jimmy, or the effects of the methane, I can't say, but I feel quite calm and peaceful. As my lamp light fades, I drift away.

Then I heard Kardac's voice.

"So perhaps another of your phobias might be explained? Trapped in a coal mine: quite similar to your dreams of confinement and claustrophobia. Could these not be past life experiences now manifesting themselves in your subconscious mind? We are all part of one magical universe, each connected to our past and our future."

"I am beginning to believe so, even though it contradicts all of my logical conditioning."

Richard Preece

"Cast logic aside; it was created by man and serves little purpose other than to incarcerate us. Let your spirit guide you. It was created by God and is the only truth."

"What of the woman? I've now loved and lost twice. What does that mean?"

"Simply that you have yet to meet your true love at your destined time."

I paused for a moment to think over Kardac's words before realizing the lateness of the hour.

"Well, I have to be going, as I have a busy day at work tomorrow."

"Then I will wish you a good night until next week for our final session."

Chapter Eleven

HARRY PRYCE

(1897–1917)

DURING THE FOLLOWING WEEK, I REGULARLY FOUND myself thinking about the two women in my past lives. They seemed quite similar in appearance and personality. Both had long dark hair, green eyes, and a voluptuous figure. Both were warm, loving, and a joy to be around. They both felt like they would be just perfect partners for me.

I realized I was starting to believe in my past lives and accept that the protagonists could have actually been me! For someone who had always been religiously agnostic and highly cynical of spiritual beliefs, this was a profound shift, and quite a shock to my system.

My nightmares involving confined spaces and falling from great heights completely ceased. I still, however, had the dreams of knives or swords and being impaled, but also now had repeated dreams in which the women appeared. Although they were brief, they were emotionally intense and quite sensual.

The woman I had seen a week or so prior as I was leaving Kardac's office also appeared in a dream. We were sitting side by side on the Malvern Hills, holding hands while gazing out across the countryside. We did not speak but simply sat close together. That too felt warm and comforting.

I arrived at Kardac's office right on time. He told me that he had another client immediately after our session, so apologized in advance that we would need to end on time.

Without further conversation, we began our regression. By then being quite accustomed to the process, it was only a few minutes before I was drifting into another place and time.

"Get yer 'ed down 'arry!"

I hear the rat-a-tat of a heavy machine gun as bullets whistle over my head. I'm lying flat in mud that smells like rotting meat. A hand grabs my arm and pulls me to the side.

"We'm better off 'ere til they reload. No sense gettin' cut to pieces."

I look at the lad next to me, also lying flat in the shell hole. I recognize his face as that of a close friend.

"Right, Jamie, we'll 'ang on 'ere a minute, though it stinks like shite."

"That be the dead Jerry over there." He points to the back side of the hole. There lies a mangled body missing an arm and with the face half eaten by rats. I nearly throw up, but hold it back and swallow hard.

Shells are now whistling overhead from our trench mortars. The earth shakes as they explode only twenty yards or so in front of us. I count at least thirty shells and then silence. The machine gun has stopped, and as the smoke shifts over us, I hear the groans and screams coming from the enemy trench. A whistle blows, and we automatically lift ourselves up from the mud and clamber out from the stinking shell hole. As we move forward at a quick step, there to either side is the rest of C Company, moving forward with fixed bayonets.

Shots ring out from the enemy trench, and I look to my side to see Nicky drop to the ground. I immediately stop to check on him. He's been hit in the arm; it is not a fatal wound but incapacitating for today's charge. I pull out a small bandage and tie it round his upper arm to slow the flow of blood.

"Watch out, 'Arry!" Nicky screams, pointing behind me with his good arm.

I turn as a German is coming straight for us, his bayonet pointed at my chest. Leaping to my feet, I parry his first thrust, and jab with all my weight into his stomach. I feel it slide through his uniform as I thrust harder to slice into his belly, then jerk upward with all my might towards his heart. But then my bayonet sticks in his rib cage and I cannot pull it out.

The scene fades away and I'm now sitting with a paintbrush in my right hand, leaning over a small white porcelain figure of a bird. It's a bullfinch. I look around to see about ten others sitting in similar positions, some painting porcelain figures and others plates.

"You're daft as a duck, 'Arry Pryce. You'm painting a bull-finch wiv yellow paint! Silly thing you!"

I turn towards the voice on my right to see a sweet-looking young girl with her dark brown hair pulled up in a tight bun. She winks at me and then blows me a kiss.

"But I still luvs yer, my little sweetheart." She smiles warmly.

"That's my girl, Esther. You always was a better painter than me. I'm a clumsy oaf with the brush and me 'ands are useless at times."

"They ain't useless when they's stroking me! Hah!" She gives me a suggestive grin.

A shrill whistle blows, and everyone around me sets down their paintbrushes.

"Fountain then, luv?" Esther asks.

"Works for me, sweetheart. Could murder a pint."

As we walk across the narrow street towards the Fountain Inn, I look up and down at the red brick terraced houses lining both sides. There's a woman in a pinafore standing on a front doorstep waving towards me.

"Yer mum wants you, 'Arry! Better see what she wants, and I'll meet yer in the bar."

"What's up, Mum?"

A tired looking older woman with greying hair greets me. "Esther's mum's not feeling well, so don't you two be staying out late tonight!"

"We won't, Mum, just a couple and I'll have her home by six."

"Alright then, 'cos she's gotta do dinner for 'er dad, and you know 'ow 'e is if 'e's kept waitin'!"

I turn and walk back to the pub to find Esther sitting at a table with two pints of beer in front of her.

"Let's go for a walk again on the Malverns this Sunday, luv. I loves it up there. Feels like a little bit of heaven to me."

"That it does, and romantic too! Nice for a cuddle in the grass."

"You devil you, 'Arry Pryce!"

"We have to be back by four though so we can get to the cathedral service. You likes that don't you."

"Aye, luv, the singing is lovely."

"Did you get the tickets for the Three Choirs yet, luv? Don't want 'em to sell out. With Elgar getting his King's award, you know it'll be popular."

"Got two tickets for his violin concerto and Vaughan Williams's *Fantasia on a Theme by Thomas Tallis*. Should be lovely."

"You're a doll! Imagine it, luv. We get to paint at the Royal Worcester porcelain works, go for walks on the Malvern Hills, and then the cathedral is just there behind where we live. We'm so lucky."

"I'm lucky to have you, Esther!"

"That you are, 'Arry Pryce, and don't you be forgettin' it!"

I hear applause—hands clapping all around—then a nudge in my side. I turn to see Esther grinning and pointing towards the stage way in front of us. Looking up and around, it takes only split seconds to recognize the high arches of the nave of Worcester Cathedral. I am at the Three Choirs Festival concert. The applause is for Edward Elgar, who is now at center stage bowing in gratitude towards the audience. As the clapping subsides, he turns towards the orchestra, surveys the musicians and nods, then raises his baton to begin the first piece of music: *Fantasia on a Theme by Thomas Tallis*. I hold Esther's hand warmly and close my eyes to soak up the beauty of the music. Tears form in my eyes as the richness of the strings seep down to my very soul.

During the intermission, Esther and I exit through the west door to sit in the gardens overlooking the River Severn.

"You can see the hills from here, luv, see?" Esther points west over the cricket ground to the Malvern Hills—just visible in the distance through the summer haze.

"Lovely view ain't it, sweetheart?"

"I know now why you goes on about that Vaughan Williams all the time; that was a beautiful bit of music, that *Thomas Tallis* thing."

"Yes, luv, it truly is. I think he might be here too today."

"Who? Thomas Tallis?"

"No silly, Vaughan Williams."

"I was just pulling yer leg, silly. I may not be educated and all that, but I knows Tallis was around in the Elizabethan days, long ago!"

I lean over and kiss her on the cheek. She blushes, lifts her shoulders, and smiles.

"We'd best be getting back in for the violin concerto," I say and start to stand up.

"Another kiss first, Harry Pryce, if you please?"

I hold her close and kiss her gently but deeply while squeezing her tight. She sighs.

"You've still got it, luv! Makes me all aquiver, it do."

The Elgar *Violin Concerto* is superb. Fritz Kreisler performs impeccably with incredible emotion. Elgar appears completely satisfied as the final chords fade into the arches. The applause is rapturous, and the whole audience stands in recognition. As the clapping fades away, my view also fades away.

"Left, left, left, right, left. About turn," a booming voice screams out as I march in time with those around me. My boots are click-clacking on the parade ground, and my arms swing back and forth in time with the sergeant major's commands.

"Halt!" he screams. "At ease! You sorry excuse for soldiers; that was pathetic! Call yourself Royal Worcester's? My grandma could do better. Hopefully you shoot a damned sight better than you parade or we're in deep trouble."

"Company dismissed! Firing range practice at fourteen hundred hours. Lee–Enfield and Vickers machine guns. One hundred rounds each."

"Crusty old shit!" I turn to see Nicky next to me, grinning as always.

"Wonder if he's ever seen action or just likes to make our lives a misery?" I reply.

"Oh, he was at Gheluvelt in 1914. Seen a lot of action, I'd say!"

"Didn't know that. Can't wait to get stuck in and see some action myself."

"Don't be wishing for something you may regret."

"Well, aren't you the sensible one, Nicky Andrews!"

"Ain't gonna be all roses," is all he says, with a fateful look about him.

"Are you thinking we made a mistake in signing up?"

"Ain't saying that. But Vesta Tilley was hard to resist. What was that thing she did? Tommy something or other? Tommy in the Trench,'" Nicky clarifies.

"Yeah, that was what got me to enlist. Well we're 'ere now for better or worse, eh?"

"'Tis true! We'll make the most as we always do, 'Arry! But I do sometimes wonder how it'll all end."

Within an hour, we are in the firing range, lying flat with Lee–Enfield 303s squeezed tightly to our shoulders.

"Ready. Aim. Fire."

A volley blasts out at the target, the recoil hitting my right shoulder hard.

"Reload and fire at will."

The clouds of smoke and the smell of gunpowder disappear.

I'm looking at a blackboard with chalk writing scrawled almost illegibly.

RWR THIRD BATTALION. JUNE 6TH, 1917.
5:00 A.M. STAND-TO-ARMS.
5:30 A.M. DAILY RUM RATION.
7:00 A.M. BREAKFAST BACON AND TEA.
8:00 A.M. WEAPON INSPECTION.
9:00 A.M. SANDBAG AND BARBED-WIRE DUTIES.
10:00 A.M. FREE TIME.
12:00 P.M. DINNER.
1:00 P.M. OFFICER INSPECTION.
5:00 P.M. STAND-TO-ARMS.
10:00 P.M. NIGHT RAIDING PARTY C COMPANY.
11:00 P.M. NIGHTTIME WATCH A COMPANY.

Just another day of monotony mixed with intermittent terror in the trenches.

"Looks like we're on raiding duty tonight, Harry." Nicky is standing next to me reading the days orders.

"Yeah, I hate raiding parties. Crawling out through the barbed wire, in the dark, never knowing what you're gonna run into. Dead bodies, rats, stinking shell holes. Then we're supposed to grab a Jerry from his trench and drag him back for interrogation. Makes no sense to me. Oh what a lovely war!"

"Now who's the cynic?" Nicky says, laughing.

"Well, it's true, ain't it? Waste of time."

"Yeah, but don't forget, raiding parties get special rations. Instead of that 'Hindenburg Fat' of turnips and sawdust, we'll get horse meat and nettles!"

"Oh right, nice fresh stinging nettles. What a delight."

"Plus, we get extra portions of Tickler's Plum and Apple jam. Mind you, I prefers the gooseberry and rhubarb any day."

"Next, you'll be relishing the tea that tastes like every other thing that's been cooked in the pot. Never before tasted tea like it! More like rat's piss to my mind."

"Likely is! Enough rats round here to sink a ship. Feasting on dead bodies, they're fat little fuckers."

"Don't get me started, Nicky. Forget the rats, at least you can see 'em. It's the lice that I can't stand, creeping and a crawling all over you."

"Hah! Then how's about the cholera and dysentery: shitting through a sieve all day long? Been more die from that than Jerry bullets, I'd say."

"And you'd be right, Nicky!"

"How's your trench foot doin' by the way?"

"Got me some new socks from Mum, so doing a whole lot better."

We both turn as Jamie Day screams out behind us.

"It's alright, Jamie, nothing to be afraid of." Nicky reaches over and pats him on the shoulder.

Nicky, Jamie, and I had all gone to school together. We were best friends. Jamie had lost it after the first few weeks of constant bombardment. He'd scream in terror at the slightest noise. He'd seen the medic, but they just called it "NYD," Not Yet Diagnosed, and sent him back to the trenches. Poor sod.

"Let's 'ave a cuppa and a game of Crown and Anchor?" Nicky suggests.

With a nod, I go and fetch the primus and get set making some tea. As the water starts to boil, I know it's going to taste like crap, but what can you expect using water scooped from a shell hole?

Crown and Anchor's a good game though and passes the time. It's a simple game; we take a bit of cloth and mark the six symbols on it with wax. Crown, anchor, club, heart, spade, and diamond. The game's all about putting your bets on your symbol of choice, then rolling the dice to see which symbol wins. Simple! We'll play it for hours, but then what else is there to do?

We're in the midst of Crown and Anchor and swigging down our tea when the padre comes walking down the trench, stepping carefully on the duckboards and avoiding the mud.

"Morning to you, lads!" He greets us with a smile.

"Morning padre!" we all chime in.

"Gambling's the devil's work!" he chastises us. Then he smiles. "But there be a lot of the devil's work around here, and I'm thinking that a game of Crown and Anchor be a small thing that the Lord will not take unkindly to. To be sure!" he adds in his thick Irish brogue.

"Want to join us, padre?" Nicky jokes.

"No, thank you for the offer, but I've some business farther up the trench. Young Bobby Jones took a bad one last night on the raiding party, and he's not long for this world. I've the last rights to ordain."

"Oh, right, poor old Bobby took one in the gut. Nasty slow death that is. I feel bad for Bobby. He's only seventeen and a nice kid. Never had much of a life and now never will. Sad."

The padre takes his leave, and we watch as he resumes his walk along the duckboards towards his grim mission.

"Got a lot of respect for them Catholic padres," Nicky adds. "Not of that persuasion myself, but our Anglican priests hide out in the safety of the support trenches while the padres are here on the front line. Gotta give it to 'em. They're here where they're needed."

"I'm with you, Nicky!"

It's now dark and we're gathering for the nighttime raiding party. Nicky, Jamie, and I are on the top step peering over the parapet into the darkness, waiting for the order to proceed.

"Wanna fag, 'Arry? Could be your last un?"

"You've a sick sense of humor, Nicky Andrews. But I'll 'ave one."

Handing out a Woodbine to me and Jamie, he strikes a Swan Vestas match, lights Jamie's smoke, and then strikes a second for mine. He's just about to strike the third, when I grab his hand and stop him.

"Third light, Nicky! What you thinking?"

"Oh shit! Right. First light they see you, second light they aim, and third light they fire. Thanks, 'Arry!"

He takes my cigarette and uses it to light his own.

"Right lads. Ready to go over and grab a Jerry?" Sergeant Hawkins is now next to us on the parapet.

"Ready as we'll ever be," Nicky murmurs.

We slide over the top of the trench into no-man's-land. Three smoke shells explode above us as we slither along like snakes on our chests. The mud stinks. Keeping my head down is hard, as I can't see where I'm going. The enemy trench is a mere fifty yards ahead, but it feels like miles crawling in the darkness. We get tangled in barbed wire, then working our way through, the enemy trench is right before us. I can hear muttering just a few yards ahead.

"Right lads, when the next shell explodes, we jump down into their trench and grab the first one we see and drag him back," Sergeant Hawkins whispers.

I look up as a smoke shell explodes above us, then jump to my feet and charge over the edge of their parapet and slide down into the trench. I almost land on top of a sleeping soldier. Still half asleep, he looks at me with total shock. I grab him while Nicky and Jamie point their Enfields at his mates. Sergeant Hawkins helps me pull him up out of the trench, and we hustle him back to the safety of our frontline trench.

We are greeted by steaming hot tea and pats on the back as our prisoner is handcuffed and pushed into the officers' dugout.

"Poor sod! They'll have him awake all night with constant questions, and likely he knows nowt!"

"Join us for a singsong lads?" a smiling face invites us, but we're all beat and ready for hard-earned sleep.

"Thanks, Billy, but I'm for shut-eye, while I can get it. I hear our next big push is coming soon enough." Pulling my greatcoat over me and tipping my helmet down over my face, I drift off into fitful sleep.

But I'm soon woken by the singing down the trench. I sit up and pull my poetry book out of my backpack. Opening up to where my page is marked by Esther's photo, I give it a kiss and settle in to write about our evening escapade.

The lads go through the usual medley: "Daisy, Daisy" / "Sweet Little Dicky Bird" / "Two Lovely Black Eyes," and finishing up with "It's a Long Way to Tipperary."

As the singing fades away, I reach back into my pack for two small books—my two favorite poems written by fellow trench dwellers.

First, I read "The Soldier" by Rupert Brooke.

If I should die, think only this of me:
That there's some corner of a foreign field
That is for ever England. There shall be
In that rich earth a richer dust concealed;
A dust whom England bore, shaped, made aware,

Gave, once, her flowers to love, her ways to roam;
A body of England's, breathing English air,
Washed by the rivers, blest by suns of home.
And think, this heart, all evil shed away,
A pulse in the eternal mind, no less
Gives somewhere back the thoughts by England given;
Her sights and sounds; dreams happy as her day;
And laughter, learnt of friends; and gentleness,
In hearts at peace, under an English heaven.

Then, in the glow of the predawn light, I read Wilfred Owen's
"Anthem for Doomed Youth."

What passing-bells for these who die as cattle?
Only the monstrous anger of the guns.
Only the stuttering rifles' rapid rattle
Can patter out their hasty orisons.
No mockeries now for them; no prayers nor bells;
Nor any voice of mourning save the choirs,
The shrill, demented choirs of wailing shells;
And bugles calling for them from sad shires.

What candles may be held to speed them all?
Not in the hands of boys, but in their eyes
Shall shine the holy glimmers of goodbyes.
The pallor of girls' brows shall be their pall;
Their flowers the tenderness of patient minds,
And each slow dusk a drawing-down of blinds.

As it's now not long until morning Stand-to-Arms, I close
my eyes, and thinking of Esther, drift off to sleep.
    I wake up with a start, a hand is shaking my shoulder.

"Don't be drifting off, Harry Pryce, we will be on our merry way before long." It is Captain Sedgwick crouching down on one knee in the shell hole by my side.

"Aye, sir, sorry 'bout that!' I say and then salute.

"I'll be leading you fine lads today. Proud to have the privilege to fight alongside you. God bless us all; we will surely need it."

"What day is it, sir?" I ask.

"June 7th, 1917. Why on earth do you ask?"

"Wasn't sure, sir. Today's my fiancé's birthday."

"Well, Pryce, you'll be seeing her soon, I'd venture."

He looks at his watch and counts down with his head nodding each number from ten. As he counts one, the earth moves, then shudders as a multitude of vast explosions blows columns of rubble high into the air just a hundred yards ahead of us.

"On the dot! 3:10 a.m. Nineteen mines should do the job." Captain Sedgwick sounds quite elated.

Within seconds, the creeping barrage commences. Shells fly over our heads, whistling and whining as they devastate the enemy front lines. The barbed wire ahead of us has all been nicely cut the past few days, so we should be clear to move at a good pace.

"Right lads, off we go! For England and Saint George," Sedgwick screams, then blows his whistle, holding it between his lips as he leaps up and waves his pistol towards the German lines.

It's funny how I'd been worrying myself to death the past few days about this moment, but now that it was here, I just felt calm. Jumping up, I move forward at a trot with all my friends alongside me. My "Brothers in Arms."

The smoke gets in my eyes, and I have to concentrate hard to make sure I don't trip and fall. To our right side I can hear the rumbling of our tanks as they give us protection. Above our heads, the shells continue to fly.

After a good fifteen minutes' trot, my heart is pounding. The smoke clears ahead of us as our lads take the first trench with little resistance.

Nicky and I clamber across the wreckage, making a bridge over the trench, and keep moving to the second trench.

Within fifty yards of the second line, the machine guns fire up. Nicky slows suddenly, then falls, grabbing his right arm.

"Holy shite, 'Arry, I'm hit!" he screams as he collapses to the ground.

I stop and lean down to see to him. Blood pours through his sleeve. I pull off my backpack and reach into the side pocket for a bandage. I wind it tightly around his upper arm to slow the flow.

"I'll be alright, 'Arry, ain't no mortal wound, but I'd best stay here for the medics."

I pat his head, grab my rifle, and turn towards the German line.

"Watch out, 'Arry!" Nicky screams.

A German soldier with fixed bayonet is charging straight for me. I instantly parry his initial jab; then swinging his rifle aside, I lunge hard and fast into his belly, hitting home. But he is swinging his rifle around towards me. As I try to pull my bayonet out, it sticks in his ribs. I feel a dull pain as his bayonet slides into my chest. I cannot stop it as it goes deeper and deeper.

We both fall to the ground, still locked together. He is fading fast and offers no more fight. I let go of my rifle and push his rifle away and the bayonet out of my chest. But I know I'm done for.

I crawl back towards Jamie and we lie side by side.

"You saved my life, Harry Pryce. He'd have finished me off for sure. But look at you; you're bleeding bad."

"Do me a favor, Jamie, give this to Esther please." I reach my shaking hand into my inside pocket and pull out my letter to Esther—the letter I'd hoped she'd never have to read.

I reach in my pocket one last time and hold her photo closely before my eyes.

I came to with tears running down my cheeks and pulled out my handkerchief to wipe my eyes.

"Well, James, what do you make of that?" Kardac inquired with a strange smile.

"Another woman and another untimely death. I don't know what to make of it?"

"Consider then that you have now experienced three souls being given up for selfish reasons and three lives being given up for selfless reasons. Doesn't that say something?"

"I know it should mean something, but right now, I don't know what!" I was exhausted from the experience and perplexed by the dilemma.

"Well, unfortunately, we will have to continue our examination in another session as my next client will be shortly arriving."

"Can we meet on Monday? I don't think I can wait until our regular day next Thursday."

"Of course. I'll mark you in my calendar now. See you Monday then. Don't fret, as I believe all will come clear when we talk next. I am confident that I have an explanation that will put your mind at rest."

"Thank you, Mr. Kardac." I shook his hand and left the office.

Walking down the stairs, I passed his next client on her way up. It was the woman!

"Excuse me?" I said as we were standing together on the same step.

"Yes?" she replied with a pretty smile.

"Have we met before? I feel as though I know you from somewhere."

"I don't think so? But I will compliment you on a good pickup line!" She laughed.

"Oh!" was all I could say as I blushed and continued my way down the stairs.

That evening, at home, I listened to all ninety minutes of Mahler's *Second Symphony* and finished my bottle of Ardbeg. Known as the *Resurrection Symphony*, it suited my mood and frame of mind perfectly. Although it was intended to portray the afterlife, to me, that evening, it portrayed the pains of past lives and the hope of future lives.

Chapter Twelve

AFTER THE SESSION, I WAS THOROUGHLY EXHAUSTED AND feeling as if my mind had been sucked out, leaving an indescribable emptiness. I drove through the rush hour traffic, hardly noticing my surroundings and fellow humans heading home to their normal and predictable lives. My life had become quite the opposite: nothing felt normal or predictable anymore. I wondered whether I should not have allowed myself to be drawn into what had become a vortex. Too many questions flooded my mind. Was any of this real? Did it truly happen, or was I simply projecting my imagination? I had confirmed that the first three people who appeared in my recollections really existed, but were their lives anything close to how I related them during my hypnosis? I just couldn't know.

Arriving home, I picked up my mail, dropped it on the kitchen counter, and went straight to my liquor cabinet. Pouring myself a liberal measure of Ardbeg Cask Strength, I added a healthy dash of water, and headed for my favorite chair on the patio outside overlooking my backyard.

Slumping down, I sipped my drink and looked out at my garden. The sun peeking through the clouds cast a glow across the flowers. My shoulders dropped as the Ardbeg warmed my stomach and quietened my thoughts. The foxgloves were in full bloom with bumblebees hovering and humming around them. I soaked up the beauty and the vibrant colors. Cobalt blue delphiniums rose above pink and purple clumps of petunias. My roses were in their full glory: yellows, sunset oranges, pinks, and deepest scarlets. It was a visual feast of color, calming my spirit and settling my mind.

With bees buzzing and chaffinches chirping, it was the epitome of a perfect English garden evening.

I wondered if Jack Price had a garden such as this at Price Manor.

Another snippet of whiskey. Then I set my glass down and closed my eyes to soak in the sounds. Sleep came upon me quickly and naturally as it took me away to a whole different place.

I'm peering through a narrow slit, metal all around me, encasing me. My hands are tightly gripping two levers, shifting slightly right then left as I feel a deep grumbling below me. Through the narrow view, I see buildings—no, more like ruins—all around. Devastation.

"Driver, hard right when I say." Rattling noises and then explosions.

"Driver, now!" Pulling hard on my right lever and pushing forward on my left, my view shifts quickly to see the back of a tank a mere twenty yards ahead.

"Gunner, aim and fire at will!"

I brace myself for the inevitable recoil and the deafening blast of the gun. As the smoke clears, our gunner has already reloaded and unleashed another shell. Each directly hits the back of the tank. Then silence for a second, followed by an enormous explosion as the tank before me disappears into flames and billowing black smoke. A hand reaches out of the hatch but never reaches the daylight.

Richard Preece

"You got them, gunner! Well done, Jonesy!"

As the smoke clears, my view shifts, and I am now looking at a narrow bridge. Another tank in front of me. Rumbling sounds surround me. I hear the whine of aircraft engines. The bridge sways and disappears, transforming into a wall and a broken-down gate that we are passing through. Before me are hordes of what look like skeletons wandering aimlessly. Then I see bodies strewn everywhere.

"Halt, driver! Tank crew dismount."

I pull myself out of my seat and clamber up through the tiny gap into the upper tank. Pulling myself out of the hatch, I suck in a deep breath of air and immediately vomit. The stench is obnoxious.

I awakened in a flash to the recognition that it was now past twilight and the bees and birds all gone. As I reached into my pocket and pulled out my handkerchief to wipe the perspiration from my brow, my mind clears. What was that and where did it come from? But I already knew.

My dad was a tank driver in World War II. He rarely shared stories of his experiences, largely I long ago concluded because he repressed them, as they were too hard for him to face. He was only seventeen years old when he enlisted, and I could not imagine how anyone at such a young age could handle what he must have seen and lived through. He once said to me on one of the few occasions he talked about the war, "Had some great friends, but most of them never made it." To me that said it all. Seeing our friends die next to us, often in pain and agony, is not something that anyone who has not experienced it can imagine.

"I've got to go and see Dad," I said out loud.

Finishing my whiskey, I put the glass on the kitchen counter and went straight to bed. Thankfully, it was a deep and peaceful sleep with no dreams.

The morning was a new day—a perfect English late summer morning, clear and crisp with a hint of chill in the air.

After a quick breakfast, I hopped in the car and headed south to Worcester. Pulling out of the driveway, I selected an eight-track and roared off listening to the opening of Pink Floyd's *Atom Heart Mother*—just right for my mood.

The M5 was clear. I floored the Jag and hurtled along as the urban sprawl quickly morphed into the rural Worcestershire landscape. Before I knew it, I was pulling off the motorway and wending my way through the northern suburbs, past where my Gran and Grandad lived, over the river, and on to St. John's. I turned into the close and pulled up right at their front door.

Mum met me at the front door and gave me a big hug.

"Who's that?" my dad's voice growled from the living room. He rarely left his armchair, spending most of his time polishing off book after book whilst puffing away on his pipe.

"You'll never guess!" Mum replied as I sauntered into the living room.

"Well, I'll never!" My dad was clearly surprised, and then I too was equally surprised as he got up and gave me a kiss on the cheek and a hefty bear-like hug. Unlike the dad I grew up with, he'd mellowed tremendously since he retired just the year before.

Growing up felt like boot camp with my dad. I swear he still thought he was in the army and treated my brother and me like squaddies. "Get your hair cut. It's over your ears and you look like a girl," he'd say. One time I'd been out at a party in the countryside and stayed the night, as nobody in their right mind was driving back into town. Arriving home the following morning, all he had to say while pruning his roses was, "Well, you'd better call the police and tell them you're alive." Classic Dad. Of course, he hadn't called the police; it was just his way of reprimanding me. On that occasion I think I earned it!

While Mum put the kettle on, I sat down at the living room table and had a good chat with Dad. I was eager to tell him about my dreams from the night before. He'd never shared much about his experiences in the war, which I understood, as they were probably something he would rather not think about. But my dreams stirred him up, and he went into a lengthy description of his war years. I knew he'd enlisted under age at seventeen and that he was a tank driver, but that was about all.

"I did my basic training in Bovington. One thing I remember well was the Morse code training. We became 'tap tap' idiots, almost losing speech capability. Sad to say, now I don't even remember the alphabet codes. After that, we did more training in Dorset and gunnery practice in Lulworth Cove. We had Sherman tanks then. A few months later we were shipped up to Kirkcudbright in Scotland for more live ammo training. Then a few weeks later we were off down to Southampton, destined to join the Eleventh Armored Division in Flanders. What a crossing that was! The weather was somewhat rough, to say the least, and the flat-bottomed barges were standing up on their sterns and smashing down. I thought the bottom would come through anytime.

"We were quickly equipped with Cromwells; very nippy cross-country tanks with a Rolls-Royce Meteor engine; beauty it was. But the armor and gun, as with most Allied tanks, was rather inadequate against Tiger and Panther front armor and their deadly eighty-eight millimeter guns. Which we would learn later!

"Racing across northern France, I recall the white or pink fine powdery dust, which burnt your eyes even with goggles on and dried your throat. The calvados opened up both of them! I will never forget taking a mug of this fluid thinking it was cider and having a good swallow before I realized; never did that again, just sipped with respect. The locals were lovely. They would stop us and hand bottles of champagne up to us as we drove through the countryside.

"The Eleventh Armored Division was given orders to take Amiens. Which, by the way, was deep in German territory. It was a long slog. Driving through northern France was like the apocalypse, hardly a house left standing, the roads nonexistent or strewn with damaged and ditched vehicles. We were driving nonstop until we reached the outskirts of Amiens. Monty must have outfoxed the Jerries because they were totally unprepared as we moved into the town. We took control within a few hours!

"Some Shermans and our Cromwells were positioned on the high ground overlooking Amiens. We got the order to stand down and were just tucking into our mess tins and having a nice cup of tea when the order changed, and we were told to take the fast route down the hill to take Amiens, much to the misfortune of our food and drink! We didn't need the intercom to tell us something was wrong; all the tins and cups ended up in the co-driver's lap!

"Then we moved on to Antwerp in Belgium and took that too by mid-September. In Antwerp, our infantry was transferred to Geneva. They had put their prisoners in the zoo cages. Needless to say, there had not been any animals about for years!

"I'm skipping the gruesome bits along the way, but I can tell you it was no easy sailing. Lost a lot of good friends on the way.

"After Antwerp, we were to move through Holland. Along the way we had a short spell with the US 101st Airborne around Nuenen and Helmond. They were one tough bunch and had a heck of a tough time taking bridges with the German SS Panzer Divisions protecting them! I can tell you. Fearless and just a little crazy. Nice lads though.

"The Cromwell was alright but no match for the Tiger. They were so heavily armored that the only way we could get 'em was to shoot 'em right up the arse! They also outgunned us, so our only option was to sneak up on them; they were slow and hard to maneuver."

He was getting pretty worked up, like I'd never seen before. I was thoroughly enjoying it.

"It was in Dinant, December 24th, Christmas Eve, when we sneaked up on two Tigers of the Second Panzer Division. We'd flanked the town and come in from the far side, so we were right behind them. Soon as they realized, their turrets started to turn, but they couldn't get a direct shot without moving their tanks. That gave us time to move in close. It took five direct hits on each of them before their petrol tanks blew. They both went up in smoke before any of their crew could escape. Nasty way to go!"

"That sounds exactly like my dream!" I exclaimed and slapped my knees.

"It certainly does. Your bridge dream sounds like our Rhine crossing near Wesel in March 1945. Scary, that was! We had just been reequipped with Comets for the push into Germany. The bridge engineers were not at all happy with that, as with the Cromwells there was space enough on the pontoon for a slatted walkway along the side for the infantry. But the track widths on the new Comet were somewhat wider than the Cromwell. We were scraping the sides of the Bailey bridge, causing havoc; the tracks were clipping the slats and tossing them up in the air like firewood. Plus, on top of that, the pontoon was swaying in the current. Couldn't see anything from my driver's seat but the tank in front of me rocking up and down!

"We went on to capture Lübeck in May, but before that I had the worst shock of the whole war. We were across the River Aller some twenty miles south of Münster when orders came through to halt, maintain position, and not fire. All came clear when two large open cars carrying senior German officers under a white flag approached and passed down through our column. Negotiations carried on throughout the day, and we were stood down in rotation to await the outcome. We soon discovered what was happening when we got to Bergen. As we pulled towards the gates, I could just glimpse the wrought iron sign over the top: 'Belsen.'

"Your dream was right. The stench was abhorrent. All I could see were hordes of living skeletons walking towards us with their hands out like beggars. Poor buggers. Later I found out there were sixty thousand of them still alive, though barely, and another thirteen thousand corpses that we had to bury. Saddest days of my life."

"Dad, how is it possible that I could dream all that, just like I was there?"

"Ah! That I couldn't say. There's more to this world than any of us know. But let me finish my story. After the surrender, we were all moved back to England, but within a few weeks there I was in a Liberator bomber with an advance party en route to Egypt. I remember thin, trembling wings bouncing along through air pockets. We were sitting in rope netting seats. That left an impression, I can tell you!

"We ended up in Giza at night. As we were flying in, I got a view of the Sphinx and pyramids by moonlight—at night, quite something to behold. But come daylight when we got to see them close up, the illusion for me was shattered. They were all very badly worn, and spitting and stinking camels were everywhere. Still it was an experience.

"Our life in Egypt was pretty lovely though. We stayed on the shore of the Great Bitter Lake when off duty, spent our days swimming, raft sailing, and general easy living until orders came to prepare to ship out to Palestine. The day came when we said our fond farewell to Egypt, and especially the bagpipe calls of the jocks next door, and we headed over the Suez Canal and up through the Sinai Desert into Palestine. After the desert and then the twisting roads through the rocky hills, we came down into citrus groves where it had recently rained; you could almost eat the fragrance!

"Reality, as usual, took over, and here I sympathize with the lads in Northern Ireland. We had been used to hitting back hard at anything that caused us problems, but now we had to stand and take it, feeling neutered and powerless. Honestly, I was glad when they demobbed us and sent us home, even though it was an experience of a lifetime seeing the Middle East."

Mum joined us for a cup of tea, and we moved on to other topics. But later, after dinner, Dad and I shared a beer, and I told him my hypnosis stories. I was surprised that he listened so intently with a knowing look on his face. He nodded after I finished each story. When I'd finished, he sat silently, then said, "Well, I've never shared this with you, Son, but a few years back I too was having the oddest dreams; quite vivid they were. So, I did a bit of research down at the County Office of Births and Deaths and low and behold I traced our family tree all the way back to the early 1800s. Your fellows at the Trafalgar, the coal mine, and the First World War were all in the family! What do you say to that, Son?"

"I'm dumbfounded, Dad. Don't know what to think."

"Well, like I say, Son, there's more to this world than we will ever know."

Chapter Thirteen

It was Monday evening and time for my next appointment with Mr. Kardac. I had deliberately set an early time for our session, as I had a ticket for the opera at 8:00 p.m. that evening at Birmingham Town Hall and did not want to miss it. Having wrapped up my afternoon meeting on the Redditch Project with the university head of the School of Architecture and Planning, I then had ample time to drive into the city and arrived a few minutes early for my appointment. Looking at my watch, it was 4:50 p.m.

Kardac welcomed me with a smile and asked me to take a seat—no different to all of our prior sessions. However, his demeanor was changed that day. He had an air of satisfaction about him, as though he was about to share a conclusion or a revelation.

"Well, James, we have traveled quite a journey together these past few weeks. Candidly, you came to me as broken or at least a man somewhat lost. Now I see before me a different person. Where once you were distraught, you now appear calm. At the outset of our journey you were confused, whereas now, to me, you seem clear. Am I correct?"

"Well now that you put it that way, yes! It's hard for me to reflect back, but I do feel more calmness and clarity. Perhaps more so than I have in years. However, I'm still struggling to comprehend why."

"Let me elucidate. Your situation is not so unusual, in fact it is quite common. But most people do not recognize or connect as you have. I am quoting from ancient texts here…

"The human spirit is eternal. Created by God. It is the human spirit that is all-important, not this flesh that profits nothing because it will not long endure in its present form.

"But, as stated in Ephesians 6:23, the body is the battleground whereon this battle we wage against the 'principalities' and 'powers' of Satan is being fought. We have mentioned that the human spirit (that is, who 'we' really are) will of necessity follow either the sinful flesh (influenced by the devil's world and all that is in it) or the Holy Spirit. In order to fully understand the mechanics of this process, we must first consider a subject that we have so far deliberately avoided: the so-called 'soul.'

"Then, according to Genesis 2:16–17, the Lord God gave orders to the Man as follows: You may certainly eat from any tree in the garden except the tree of the knowledge of good and evil—from it you may not eat, for on the day you eat from it, you will certainly die.

"By creating a tree whose fruit was forbidden to them, God gave our first parents the option of *not* following His will, a will that clearly had only their best interests at heart, for violation and rebellion would result in immediate spiritual death.

"We have no precise information as to how long the devil waited to launch his attack. It stands to reason that, given his own experience, Satan would want to give Adam and Eve time to sin on their own. After all, the devil had done so without temptation, and we may assume that part of his defense before God had been that any sort of creature would eventually act as he had acted (that is, sooner or later fall into sin and rebellion against God). But even though Man had possessed a freedom of the will comparable to that of the angels, it soon became apparent to the devil that Adam and Eve were unlikely to sin against God—without a push.

Richard Preece

The tree of knowledge of good and evil had not the intrinsic attraction for Adam and Eve that the usurpation of universal rule had for Satan and his angels. The reason for this relative lack of interest in transgressing the bounds that God had set for them was rooted in the relative limitations of their knowledge and abilities. As terrestrial, corporeal creatures, mankind did not (and does not) possess an inherent knowledge of the spiritual realities of the universe and was at the time incapable of leaving the earth in any case. This lack of extensive and multifaceted knowledge (as possessed by the angels), coupled with the absence of angelic power and ability, thus turned out to be a strength in terms of our first parents' resistance to temptation (and is a reminder to us all that the more one has—of anything—the more tempted to arrogance one is). But every strength also has a concomitant weakness, and the devil was quick to assess the vulnerabilities of this new species.

"The essence of Satan's strategy in attacking Adam and Eve was the same then as it is now, namely, to drive a wedge of deception between the believer (or potential believer) and the truth.

"The devil's strategy as employed against Eve is thus critically important for us to understand today, for his tactics remain essentially the same: first, involve us in a 'dialogue,' some form of subtle temptation, verbal and otherwise, which engages our egos and our arrogance; second, use this dalliance with him to throw the slightest shadow of doubt upon some aspect of God's word, God's commands, or God's character. Finally, as soon as a fracture of distrust, a fissure of failing belief, appears in our shield of faith, then slam home whatever wedge will fit the crack.

"His statement that Eve and her husband would 'not die' as a result of partaking of the forbidden fruit was a compound lie. In truth, disobedience meant instant *spiritual death* (condemnation by and alienation from God), eventual *physical death* (as the process of degeneration began), and ultimate *eternal death* (in the absence of some amazingly gracious intervention by God Himself)."

"That's all very interesting, but how does it relate to me?"

"Ah! The million-pound question, as they say. What I am about to share will likely challenge your intellect, so before I begin, please focus less on your mind and more on your spirit. Allow your spirit to listen and absorb without your mind stepping in and overruling with logic. My explanation will initially sound illogical, so you must allow it to soak in before your intellect dismisses it. Can you do that?"

"I will give it my best! You've taught me to listen to my spirit and to at least consider the unimaginable. So please, proceed!"

"I will make it brief and hopefully succinct. You are, as we all are, a spirit of God. Your spirit was created by God and shall ultimately return to God. Your body is purely a physical manifestation, or a temporary home, for your spirit while you are on earth.

"With me so far?"

"Yes. Though a month ago I'd have laughed at you and walked out, today I get it."

"Good. Then listen to this. God has given you the opportunity to learn and grow through your life experiences. He is interested in your spirit and not your body. His goal is to help you become a heavenly spirit to be ready to take your place in heaven next to him. Consequently, Satan will test you and tempt you while God is guiding you along your path. Still with me?"

"So far."

"Simply put, the past life stories that you shared with me during hypnosis were all real. They all happened, just as you experienced them. Owen, Orlando, Jack, Ned, Milton, and

Harry were all real. They each passed through this world tested and tempted. Owen, Orlando, and Jack succumbed to temptation and paid the ultimate price. Ned, Milton, and Harry made the ultimate earthly sacrifice in giving up their lives that others may survive. In doing so, they unknowingly paid the debt incurred in their prior lives. The slate, as you say, was thus cleaned."

"So, you are saying that it was the same spirit through each of those lives and they responded in different ways? Being self-centered and tempted by gratification during their earthly lives or being selfless and giving up their mortal lives for others?"

"Exactly so! I could not have put it better, James."

"Incredible. It all makes sense to me now, but why then, if the slate was cleaned after Harry gave up his life in the horrors of the First World War, would I have suffered with my nightmares and come to see you?"

"That is something I cannot say. Perhaps the connections between each of the earthly life experiences needed to be made before the spiritual debt could be fully settled. There is much of God's plan that we will never comprehend."

"Thanks to you, Mr. Kardac. I feel a true sense of clarity, the likes of which I have never before experienced."

Soon after, I left his office in order to make it to the opera on time.

It was the *Barber of Seville*, not necessarily one of my favorites, but I did love Rossini. Arriving a little early, I chose to listen in on the preconcert lecture, rather than sitting in the bar. Maybe I would learn something?

Seated and waiting patiently, I noticed a young woman accompanied by two older persons, who I assumed to be parents, take a seat right in front of me. She didn't notice me, but my attention was captured by her back. Wearing a long silk evening dress, her back was fully exposed, showing a long scar. Her hair was pulled up in a neat bun, and she wore a gold necklace. Why I noticed I could not tell, but something about her drew me and continued to draw me in, as if I knew her.

The lecture was quite mundane, and the questions people asked incredibly dull. I suddenly found myself compelled to ask a question. Not in the least interested in the response, but more in an attempt to draw her attention.

"So, in his later years Rossini stopped composing liturgical pieces and concentrated on operas. His requiem *Stabat Mater* was magnificent, but that was his final composition for the church. Why was that?"

If I thought I sounded completely pompous and a total peacock posing for attention, I was!

I'm not sure I listened to the answer, as I was more mesmerized by her back. Expecting her to turn and notice me, I was disappointed. Walking out slowly, I hoped she might notice me; I was disappointed. She hesitated and talked with the lecturer. I stopped and waited. As she proceeded down the staircase, I realized I felt like a stalker and decided to give up and pass her by. Just as I passed her side, she stopped and turned towards me.

"Are you the one that asked the question about the requiem? What is a requiem? Didn't we meet outside Mr. Kardac's office?"

Quickly gathering my thoughts, I paused and then explained as eloquently as I could, attempting to sound profoundly interesting. Perhaps I succeeded, as we continued our conversation until the bell rang for the start of the opera. I shook her hand and bid her farewell.

Throughout the first act, I gave little or no attention to the music but rather planned out my next move. I would find her at the intermission!

I need not have planned, as I was walking towards the bar at the start of the break, there she was walking towards me. After offering to buy her a drink, we immediately engaged in deep conversation, which continued until the second bell.

"Are you coming to *La Traviata*?" she asked.

"I'd love to, but I might be away on business. Could I ask for your phone number just in case?"

"Of course! My name is Emily, in case you wondered," she replied with a wry smile.

"Oh, right, I didn't introduce myself. I'm James. Pleased to make your acquaintance." I sounded like I was speaking from another time; perhaps I was.

The bell rang for us to return to our seats, and so we said farewell. The remainder of the opera captured little of my attention as my mind was elsewhere, reflecting on what had just transpired. Out of the blue—it was quite shocking to me. I had never before felt quite so compelled to connect with someone and to then find the conversation flowed so easily as if we had known one another for ages. It was remarkable.

Once home, I poured myself a healthy measure of Ardbeg and settled on the patio to enjoy the evening in retrospect. Relishing in the enjoyment of meeting Emily and unwilling to let the moment pass away, I did, however, remind myself that my relationships often started out rosy, as I'd shared with Kardac at our first session. But this was different; radically so.

Chapter Fourteen

EMILY HAD HARDLY LEFT MY MIND DURING THE FOLLOWING days, but I was busy at work and also reminded myself to be a little cautious, to avoid being overly optimistic and coming across as desperate. So, it was not until Sunday that I picked up the phone and called her.

After initial trepidation, unsure if she would remember me, we fell into an incredibly easy back-and-forth conversation. Sharing openly our thoughts, our fears, our interests, after almost an hour on the phone, I realized I'd never had a telephone conversation with anyone, even my mother, longer than fifteen minutes! Yet, this felt like we were only just warming up and could have continued on for another hour without taking a breath. It simply felt as though we thought and felt alike in so many ways.

Before hanging up, we had agreed on a day out to Worcester and a walk on the Malvern Hills the following Saturday.

During our conversation, I'd learned that she was originally from Ledbury, a small medieval market town on the Herefordshire side of the Malvern Hills. She was familiar with The Prince of Wales pub—coincidentally one of my very favorites.

"Let's have lunch there!" I'd suggested with unreserved excitement.

"I would love that!"

She also shared the reason that she was visiting Kardac when we first met. Struggling, herself, with relationship failures, she felt he might be able to help uncover the reason. After two visits, she felt it was going nowhere and tired of his "psychobabble bullshit" as she called it. The only thing he concluded for her was that she would meet her life partner when destiny determined. After that she didn't return to see him.

She did add that it was not wasted, as we met because of Kardac!

That evening, after ending the day with my routine Ardbeg while sitting in the garden, and having listened to my favorite piano concerto, Shostakovich's second *Piano Concerto*, I headed up to bed.

I drifted off into a deep sleep almost immediately. I soon found myself in the midst of a vivid dream.

I am in Kardac's office, though seated in his leather chair in front me is not Kardac, but someone else. Raven black hair hangs down to his shoulder. He has dark, almost black deepset piercing eyes, quite menacing but for the fact he is smiling benevolently. Dressed in a black Victorian suit with golden brocade waistcoat and a gold watch chain draped from his chest pocket, he looks the epitome of a wealthy gentleman, though with an otherworldly air about him. Both hands rest on a silver cane in front of him as he leans forward towards me. Looking at his hands, I am taken by his finely manicured nails and a silver ring on the little finger of his right hand set with a black stone.

"You may let go now," is all he says.

Then I woke up.

It was 5:15 a.m. and though unusually early for me to get up from bed, I knew I wouldn't sleep after that dream, so I put on my dressing gown and went downstairs to make coffee.

With my coffee in my left hand and a cigarette in my right, I sat comfortably in the armchair on the patio. It was of course still dark, but for the glow of the full moon peeking between fleeting clouds. There was a predawn chill in the air, but I felt a warm glow inside as I reflected on my dream. Something about it had comforted me, but what, I could not comprehend.

The figure in my dream seemed familiar, even though I'd never seen him before. There was something about him that I knew and felt a connection to. But what, I couldn't place. Then I thought about Kardac, and closing my eyes, pictured myself sitting across from him in his office. Imagining myself back there, I started to see him quite clearly. Holding his notebook on his lap, he lifted his pen to make a note, and as he did so, my eyes focused on his hand and saw the ring. On the little finger of his right hand, clear as day, was a silver ring with a black stone. It was the same ring as in my dream!

With a jolt, I opened my eyes, reached for another cigarette, and took a gulp of lukewarm coffee. Could it possibly be? Then the lightning bolt hit me.

It was Le Ciffre in my dream. Could Kardac be Le Ciffre?

If the past few weeks had taught me anything, it was that apparently the most unbelievable things were possible and that there were more connections to past events than I would have ever imagined.

This felt like the key to it all, or the final piece of the jigsaw. I didn't know why or how, but deep down I knew it. It was then that I determined I must make another visit to Kardac, but this time it would be an unscheduled encounter.

Wednesday evening, immediately after work, I drove up to his office. This would be the first time I'd visited without an appointment, so I was somewhat apprehensive, as he could easily be out of his office or engaged in a session with another client.

Having found a parking space just down the street, I walked up with a bounce to my step, smiling and greeting passersby. Bounding up the stairs, I reached his door and knocked. No reply. I knocked again. Still no reply. Disappointed, I stepped back and started to walk away, and then looking back towards the door noticed that his name plate was gone. Odd!

Rushing back down the stairs, as I left the building, I saw the sign. "Office for Lease."

Had he closed up shop? That would be strange. I took a note of the estate agent's telephone number and looked around for a phone box. Spotting one right across the street, I reached into my pocket for change and quickly dialed the number as soon as I closed the phone box door.

It rang for just a few seconds.

"Good evening. Grant and Associates. How may I help you?" a pleasant voice greeted me.

"Hello, I'm inquiring about the office lease on Bank Street. Is it still available?"

"Let me check, sir."

After a minute or so, which felt like an eternity, she was back on the phone.

"Yes, it is. It hasn't been leased for over a year now and would be available immediately. Would you be interested, sir?"

"Are you sure of that?"

"Absolutely, sir."

I hung up in shock.

The Royal Oak pub was on the corner just across the street and that was where I was going. I needed a drink to settle me down. As my head was spinning, I was cautious crossing the street, now busy with early evening traffic. This was to be my first visit to the Royal Oak, so I had no idea what to expect, but as I pushed the door and walked in, I was pleasantly surprised by a warm and welcoming atmosphere. It was a Victorian pub with original etched mirrors behind the imposing mahogany bar and stained-glass lights hanging from the ceiling that cast a warm glow over the room. Choosing the bar, I sat myself down on a velvet upholstered stool and sighed quite loudly.

"Bad day, sir?"

"Well, *perplexing* would be the word that comes to mind."

"Then you'll be in need of a nice drink to settle your spirit, I'd say, sir?"

"Indubitably," I replied, scanning the bottles behind the bar. Not seeing Ardbeg, I chose instead Lagavulin 16. A little pricey, but the afternoon's events warranted it.

After adding a little water to open up the peat and smoky essence, I took a healthy sip and lit up a Dunhill. The warmth of the single malt calmed me down, and I settled into quiet reflection.

"There's more to this world than we will ever know." My dad's words flashed into my head.

After reliving my visit to the vacant office and reflecting back on my past few weeks' experiences, I could only conclude that Dad's words were just right. There seemed to be little to gain from analyzing and attempting to explain the incredible events of the past month. There could be no explanation!

So instead, I shifted my thoughts to Emily and the possibilities of something. Who knows what that something could be, I thought, but whatever it may turn out to be, somehow I felt it was to be special and unlike anything I had previously experienced.

Was it just a coincidence that she too visited Kardac? Or was that somehow orchestrated by the powers that be? That, I could not explain.

The following morning as I was leaving home for work, still wrapped up in my thoughts, I literally bumped into the postman.

"Morning, Mr. Price. Got a package for you here." He reached into his bag and pulled out a package wrapped in black paper tied with silver string—unlike any parcel I'd ever received.

"Thank you kindly," I replied as I took the package from his hand and returned to the house to open it without delay.

Snipping the string with scissors, I anxiously unwrapped the black paper to find a letter and a number of documents. They looked very old and faded. Unfolding the first document, it was immediately obvious that it was a contract. The edges of the paper were frayed and the writing in handwritten ink. It was the contract! Signed by Owen Rees and Bernael Le Ciffre. The second was signed by Orlando Pryce, and the third by John Price.

I steadied myself and sat down on the couch to open the letter.

"Dear Mr. Price,
Having been an honor to make your acquaintance and hopefully in some small way alleviate your suffering, it is my pleasure to inform you that the accounts of Owen Rees, Orlando Pryce, and John Pryce are, on this day the sixth of November the year of our Lord nineteen

seventy-eight, each paid in full and all previous commitments settled.

Please accept my sincere wishes for a healthy and happy future, both in this life and the next.

Yours sincerely,
Bernael Le Ciffre."

Picking up the documents, I moved outside to the patio and reread them over and over as it all started to sink in.

Chapter Fifteen

⸻

As I sat on a blanket overlooking the countryside spreading out towards the horizon, my heart glowed. I reached my hand out to be accepted and caressed. A skylark chirped high above. My spirit sang. I had found my home.

"Let's go for a beer at the Prince of Wales!" I said.

"You have my vote," she responded.

I turned and leaned towards Emily, kissing her with my very soul.

END

*"There are more things to heaven and hell
than we mere mortals can surely tell."*

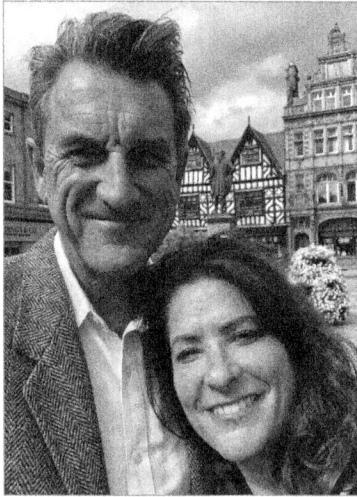

Richard Preece

.

Printed in Great Britain
by Amazon

46968557R00086